JOSH'S JUSTICE

BAD IN BOOTS SERIES

P.T. MICHELLE
PATRICE MICHELLE

LIMITLESS INK PRESS, LLC

JOSH'S JUSTICE (BOOK 4)

BY P.T. MICHELLE & PATRICE MICHELLE

BAD IN BOOTS Series
Reading Order

Harm's Hunger
Ty's Temptation
Colt's Choice
Josh's Justice

Note: Harm's Hunger is the only novella. All the other books are novel length. Every book in the series can be read as a stand alone story

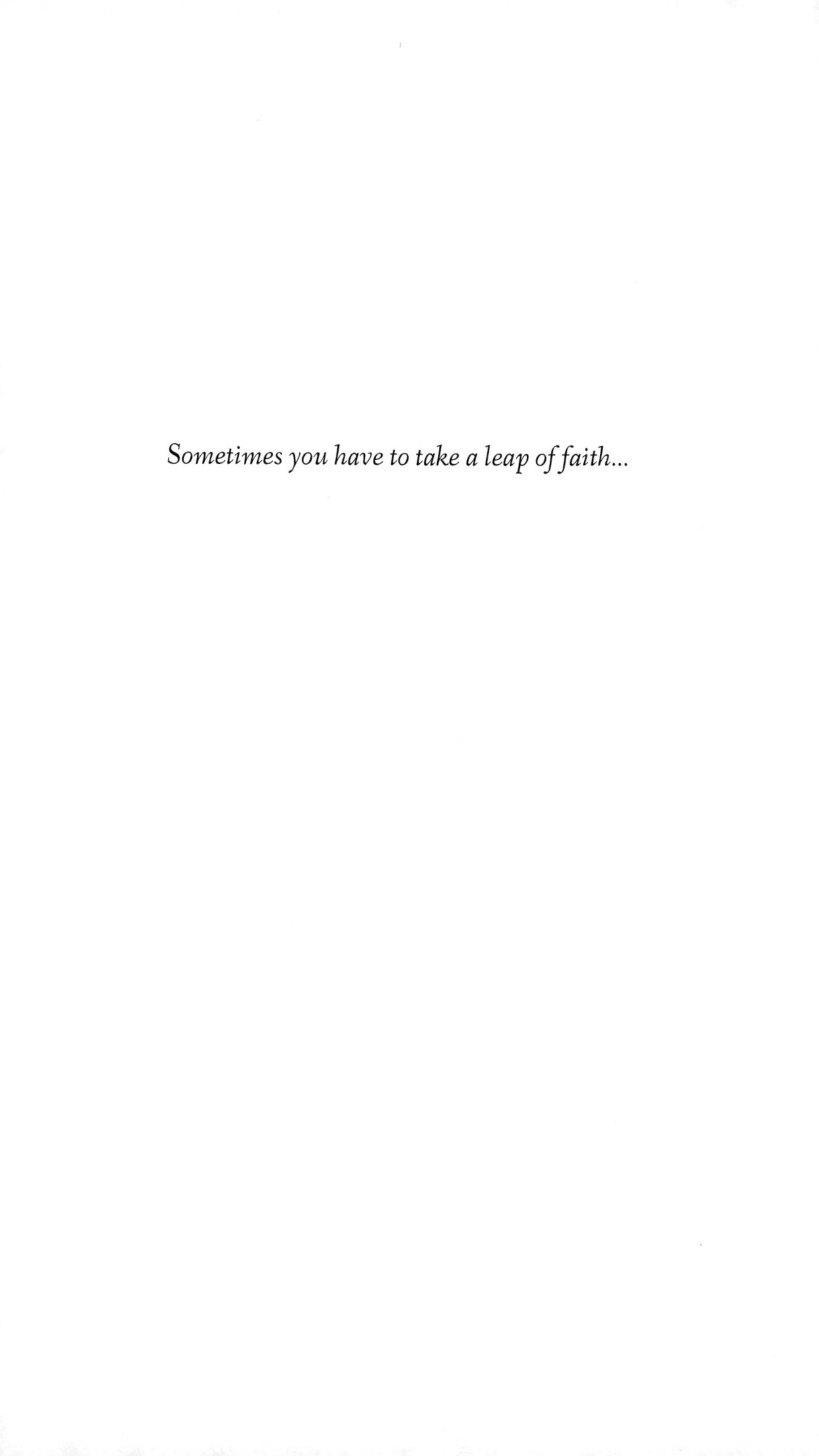

Sometimes you have to take a leap of faith...

COPYRIGHT

2013 BY P.T. MICHELLE AND PATRICE MICHELLE

Print ISBN-10: 1939672376
Print ISBN-13: 9781939672377

All rights reserved. This ebook is licensed for your personal enjoyment only. This eBook cannot be re-sold or given away to others. No parts of this ebook may be reproduced, scanned or distributed in any manner whatsoever without written permission from the author.

This is a work of fiction. Any references to historical events, real people, or real locales are used fictitiously. Other names, characters, places and incidents are the product of the author's imagination, and any resemblance to actual events, locales or persons, living or dead, is entirely coincidental.

To stay informed when the next **P.T. Michelle** book will be released, join P.T.'s free newsletter http://bit.ly/11tqAQN

SUMMARY

After Sabrina Gentry's ex-boyfriend makes her question her judgement in men, she takes a vacation to see her girlfriend in Texas with only one rule in mind: The first man who trips her trigger, she's going for it. No hesitation, no reservations, no thoughts for the future. She'll just live in the moment.

Of course, it's just her luck that the one intriguing guy she stumbles across made a pass at her thinking she was someone else. Refusing to be deterred from her new rule, Sabrina sets out to convince Josh Kelly that sometimes what you really want is standing right in front of you.

A case of mistaken identity might've introduced Josh to Sabrina, but before he can get to know the woman whose curvy backside made him lose all common sense, a near fatal accident slams them together, further heightening their fierce attraction. As Sabrina and Josh uncover layers about each other that could threaten their budding relationship, more danger lurks, waiting to strike.

The books in the BAD IN BOOTS series can be

read as stand alone stories. Reading order of the BAD IN BOOTS series, which is best suited for readers 18+:

BAD IN BOOTS Series:

HARM'S HUNGER (Book 1 - Novella)
TY'S TEMPTATION (Book 2 - Novel)
COLT'S CHOICE (Book 3 - Novel)
JOSH'S JUSTICE (Book 4 - Novel)

1

"Miss? Um, Miss?"

Sabrina turned and realized the girl at the rental car counter was calling her.

Pulling her suitcase behind her, she approached the rental car clerk. "Oh, sorry. I was just checking out the great scenery Texas has to offer," she said, smiling.

The girl followed her line of sight to the tall dark-haired guy leaning against the conveyor belt column with his phone pressed to his ear and nodded in agreement. "How can I help you?"

"I wanted to pick up my rental car." She glanced to the side as the man she'd been checking out walked over to the counter near her and asked another rental agent for a pen.

"The name?" the girl asked.

"Sabrina Gentry," she answered as the guy scrawled something on a piece of crumpled-up paper, then shoved his cell phone in his back pocket.

The clerk tapped on her keyboard and looked up, brow furrowed. "I don't have a Sabrina Gentry listed."

"But I made a reservation—" Sabrina sighed heavily. "Can you just set me up in a rental now, please?"

The girl shook her head. "I wish I could, but we just had a large group come through and they took all the available cars we have. I can have a car for you by tomorrow."

"How am I supposed to get to the Lonestar ranch?" she asked, irritated at the inconvenience.

"Robbie could take you," she suggested, "but you'd have to wait until it slowed down a bit. Probably a couple of hours."

A couple of hours? Sabrina's good mood slowly began to evaporate.

"Or we could call you a cab?"

"Ma'am?" a man said behind her.

"Yes?" Sabrina turned, surprised to see it was the guy she'd been ogling earlier.

"I couldn't help but overhear your dilemma. I'm on my way to Boone if you need a ride."

With dark wavy hair, high cheekbones and a full bottom lip, he looked even better up close. There had to be some Hispanic heritage in his very exceptional genes. Why'd her parents have to etch the safety rule "don't ever hitch a ride with a stranger" permanently inside her head?

She met his chocolate-brown gaze with an appreciative smile. "Thank you for the offer, but I'll just call my friend Elise."

"You mentioned the Lonestar. You're talking about Elise Tanner, right?"

Sabrina stared at him in confusion for a second. "Oh, sorry.

Her married name threw me. She's been Elise Hamilton to me since our college days."

"Colt and I have known each other for years," he says, extending his hand. "Dirk Chavez."

She clasped his hand and smiled. "Sabrina Gentry. Nice to meet you." *Friend by association, and therefore no longer a stranger.* "I'd be grateful for the ride. If you're sure it won't be too much trouble."

He shifted his black duffle bag to his other shoulder, then reached down and grabbed the handle of her bag. "Not at all, Ms. Gentry." Glancing at the girl behind the counter, he said, "Call the Lonestar ranch when you've located a car for Ms. Gentry."

"That's Miss Gentry," Sabrina corrected.

A wide smile spread across his lips. "I mean, Miss Gentry."

"Will do," the clerk said.

While Dirk stowed his bag in the back of his black pickup truck, Sabrina stood on the passenger side and called across the truck bed, "I can't thank you enough for the lift."

"No problem, ma'am. I live to rescue stranded women," he replied, then frowned. "Um, that came out wrong."

Sabrina laughed. "I knew what you meant. Call me Sabrina," she said, loving the respectful way Texan men spoke to their women. She had friends who'd be offended if someone called them ma'am—saying, "It makes me feel like an old woman." But when the "ma'am" came accompanied with that sexy drawl, she just melted.

"Only if you call me Dirk." His biceps flexed underneath the short sleeves of his red t-shirt as he lifted her suitcase into the truck's cab. Sabrina couldn't help but smile. *This vacation is already starting to look up.*

Dirk pulled out of the parking lot and slid his gaze her way. "Ever been to Texas before?"

Sabrina shook her head. "And I feel a little bad on the timing, to be honest."

When he gave her a curious look, she continued, "I totally forgot how newly married Elise and Colt were until after I'd called her to see if I could come for a visit." She rolled down the window to let the warm wind blow against her skin. Holding her long black hair down, she continued, "The last thing I want to do is intrude."

Dirk's eyes lit with understanding. "Colt's a down-to-earth, straightforward guy. You'll feel right at home around them. Of course Mace will be there." He turned the car onto the interstate and snorted. "I'm sure he'll keep you entertained."

He sounded amused, piquing her curiosity. "Mace?"

"Yeah, Colt's youngest brother...the consummate ladies' man."

Sabrina snickered. "Ah, now I see." *Maybe someone like Mace is exactly what I'm looking for.* No strings attached, she thought even as she checked out Dirk's muscular forearms and the defined veins running down them. *But this Dirk guy...*

"The chief called a mandatory meeting. All firefighters, get your asses down to the firehouse," the CB on the dashboard crackled, interrupting her thoughts.

While Dirk picked up the handset to respond, she sighed, her high spirits plummeting. Why did he have to be a firefighter? Why couldn't he have been a border patrol officer or an ambulance driver? *Anything* but a firefighter? Thoughts of her dad floated to the surface, but she inhaled deeply and pushed them to the back of her mind.

Placing the handset back on the CB holder, Dirk said, "Sorry, 'bout that. Duty calls, but no worries. The Lonestar's on my way."

Ten minutes later, Dirk pulled up the long drive to the Lonestar and stopped in front of the ranch house. Sabrina had jumped out of the passenger side to grab her bag, but Dirk was already there, smiling as he pulled down her suitcase and turned the handle toward her. "Delivered safe and sound." When she smiled her thanks and moved to take the handle from him, he held fast, his smile broadening. "If you do start to feel like a third wheel while you're here, feel free to call me. I'll be happy to show you around Boone."

Disappointed that she'd have to turn him down after he'd been so nice to her, Sabrina got cut off by the CB kicking off again.

"Chavez? You there?"

Taking her suitcase, she glanced at the CB. "Thanks for the lift, Dirk. I don't want to keep you from your meeting."

Dirk nodded, then rounded the truck to get back inside. As he drove off, he waved from his open window. "Take care, gorgeous."

Sabrina waved good-bye to Dirk, then turned to take in the Lonestar ranch. Green shutters and a long front porch accented a rambling white house that graced the end of the long driveway. Ten feet away from the ranch house sat a smaller version of the large house. A barn and stables led into gated open pastures that seemed to go on forever.

"There you are!" Elise called from the open screen door at the main house before she skipped down the porch steps. "I was getting worried about you." Hugging her friend, she glanced around. "Where's your car? I heard one pull up."

Sabrina sighed. "Speedy Rental didn't have a car available for me yet, so I hitched a ride here with Dirk Chavez."

"I told you not to bother with a rental. So, Dirk, hug?" Elise grinned. "How'd you manage that?"

"Dumb luck? He'd just arrived at the airport and overheard where I was going when Speedy Rental fell through."

Elise pouted dramatically. "And here I thought it was something more interesting, like you tripped him to get his attention, or dazzled him with your gorgeous self."

Sabrina glanced down at her low-riding jean shorts and casual green tank top, before meeting her friend's teasing gaze with a wry smile. "I don't think this Plain Jane-ness had anything to do with it. I believe it was his fireman's rescuer nature that made him offer me a ride."

"Ah." Elise hooked her arm with Sabrina's and led her toward the house.

When Sabrina sighed and turned to stare at the beautiful rolling pastures surrounding the ranch, Elise asked, "You're thinking about your dad, aren't you?"

She met Elise's green gaze. "It's been almost ten years, but it still hurts. The CB call in Dirk's truck brought it all back."

Elise took her suitcase from her and set it on the porch. Wrapping her arm around Sabrina's shoulders, she started toward the stables, leading Sabrina along. "Your dad wouldn't want you to be sad, Bri. He loved you with all his heart. Did I ever tell you he told me that?"

Stopping mid-stride, Sabrina glanced at her friend. "He said that to you?" She knew he loved her, but her father rarely discussed his emotions.

Elise nodded. "He told me while we were sitting in the dorm room your first day at college. You and your mom had gone shopping to stock the fridge. Maybe it was easier for him to talk to someone he didn't know very well. I think he was feeling sad that he was losing you to the next stage in your life and he didn't know how to express that to you, so he told me."

"Why didn't you tell me?" Sabrina couldn't believe Elise had never told her this.

Elise squeezed her shoulder and continued walking them toward the stables. "Because you lost your dad that very next day. I thought I'd wait until you were over his death, but as time went on, it seemed you just became very sad whenever you thought of him. If his name came up you'd be depressed for days. I didn't want to contribute to that."

"Why tell me now?"

"Because I'm older and hopefully wiser, and I realize that you need to hear just how much your dad loved you. He wanted you to be happy. He said that's what he lived for...to make sure his little girl was the happiest she could be in life."

Tears gathered and Sabrina swiped them away. Her dad's death in that downtown building fire had gutted her. She'd lost him too soon. The fact she didn't get the chance to say goodbye had left her in a kind of heavyhearted limbo. She used to dream about him...about waiting to say goodbye, but she rarely had that dream any more. Even though she still missed him terribly, Elise's words smoothed over her frazzled emotions.

Wrapping her arm around Elise's trim waist, she hugged her back. "Thanks for letting me come for a visit and for finally sharing what my dad said to you. It does help a little."

Elise squeezed her shoulder. "That's what friends are for, to pick you up and cheer you on."

As they entered the stables, Elise called out to a man who'd just ridden in from the pastures. "Hi, honey. Come meet my college roommate, Sabrina."

A rugged-looking, dark-haired man with deep blue eyes dismounted from his horse. His scuffed, dusty boots stirred the dirt floor as he walked over, pulled off his cowboy hat, and put out his hand. "Colt Tanner. Nice to meet you, Sabrina. Welcome to the Lonestar."

When Sabrina smiled and took his hand, he put his hat back on and glanced between the two women, amazement dawning in his eyes. "Other than a slight difference in height, it's uncanny how much you two look alike."

Elise nodded and let go of Sabrina to step into her husband's embrace. "Yeah, while we were in college, even though Sabrina's complexion is a bit darker than mine, people mistook us for sisters all the time, and if they were drunk, twins."

Colt kissed his wife on the forehead, saying in a gruff tone, "Darlin', I could spot you from behind in a crowd of three hundred."

Sabrina grinned at the love and sheer "knowing" that reflected in his gaze when he looked at Elise. "Oh, to be so devoted in love," she sighed dramatically.

"Dirk's available," Elise said with a sly look."

Sabrina stiffened. "I'm nowhere near ready to settle down yet."

As she spoke, another man on horseback trotted into the stables, his brown cowboy hat pulled low over his face.

"Well, then, *do* I have the man for you." Elise swept her arm in the man's direction as he approached. "Sabrina, meet Mace Tanner."

Mace walked his horse close and pulled off his hat. Looking down at her, he said, "Welcome to the Lonestar, Sabrina." His tousled light brown hair, square jaw, and beautiful green eyes would snag any woman's attention. Leaning on his saddle horn, Mace held her gaze, his full of devilish mischief. When she blinked first, he winked and grinned. "I promised Elise I'd take you on a tour when you were ready. How about now?"

Sabrina cast Elise a nervous glance. "I've never ridden a horse before."

"This is your welcome." Mace put his hand out. When she put hers in his, expecting him to shake it, he held fast and looked at Colt. "Give her a boost, bro."

Before Sabrina could decline, Colt had grabbed her around the waist and lifted her up on the horse in front of Mace. "Enjoy your tour," he said, then shot his brother a meaningful stare. "Behave."

Mace gave a deep laugh and turned the horse around. As they walked out of the stables, the unfamiliar, swaying movement made Sabrina tense. Gripping the saddle horn for support, she tried not to let her anxiety show.

Once they'd reached the open fields, Mace wrapped an arm around her waist. "Relax, Sabrina," he said, amused. "It's half the battle in learning to ride a horse."

As Mace urged his horse into a trot and then a full gallop, taking off across the green pasture, Sabrina forced her mind not to think about falling and being trampled by hooves.

After a while, Mace slowed his horse to an easy pace and pointed out different sections of the Lonestar ranch where the cattle and horses grazed.

The moment he started to pull his arm away from her waist, Sabrina clasped his hand and held it in place. She did *not* want to fall off this horse.

Mace wrapped his arm around her waist once more, pulling her against his chest. "Better?" he asked in a soft tone.

Sabrina nodded. "Why do I get the feeling you don't mind a bit?"

"'Cause I don't, darlin'. Not at all."

"So I've heard. Your reputation precedes you, Mace Tanner."

"Ah, someone's been talking about me." His tone dropped to a seductive whisper. "I hope it was all good."

"Considering my source was a man, er...I hope not," she teased.

"No worries there." He adopted a smug smile. "Must've been jealous."

"Are you always so sure of yourself?" she asked, both intrigued and entertained by his sexy confidence.

"Why not?" His shoulders moved behind her in a shrug. "I have nothing to lose."

Sabrina shot a huge smile over her shoulder. "I like your attitude."

Mace eyed her, then chuckled. "I think we're going to get along just fine, Sabrina. Elise tells me you're here for a week."

"Yeah, I'm taking some time away from work to relax and um...find my inner self." Schooling her features, she couldn't help thinking about her two cousins. They would be howling with laughter if they'd heard her comment. It was their idea—actually, it was a three-way bet between them—that sometime this summer, they'd throw caution in the wind and have a fling. What would Elise think of her plan?

Spreading his hand across her rib cage, Mace drew his own conclusions as to her meaning. "Just let me know if you're up for it. I'll be glad to help find out exactly what makes you purr."

His comment made her heart beat faster, but underneath that irresistible sexy confidence, her instincts told her Mace always held a part of himself back. She recognized that attribute well, since she'd perfected it.

She smirked. "I'll keep that in mind."

Mace nodded and returned to his tour guide duties. "Ever been on a ranch before?"

She shook her head.

Turning his horse toward a different pasture, he said, "Let's go meet some of the Lonestar ranch hands. They'd love to tell a beautiful woman all about what they do on a daily basis."

"And what do you do? Well, besides flirt outrageously with your female guests."

"You mean there's more to life?" A shocked look crossed his face before he sobered. "I help run the ranch, but I spend most of my time marketing the rodeo side of the Lonestar. What about you? What do you do when you're not flirting with men you've just met?"

"Touché." Sabrina loved that Mace gave as good as he got. "When I'm not taking a long overdue summer vacation, I help run an advertising agency in Arizona."

"Darlin', we should definitely exchange notes," he commented, his tone more than a little suggestive as his grip on her waist tightened briefly.

"You are too much," she shot back.

"I'm a man. You're a gorgeous woman. I'd be a fool not to try." He shrugged, completely unrepentant.

"I imagine it'd be so easy to fall under your spell." She gave a soft laugh. Mace's compliment really boosted her spirits. She'd taken this vacation to get away. Her confidence had really taken a beating with Jeremy's rejection. He'd broken up with her, claiming that she was too rigid, and that she tried too hard to control every aspect of her life, even him.

She'd been so careful in dating, passing on a lot of date opportunities over the years. She'd rather be alone than go out just for the sake of going out. Then she met Jeremy. They'd been together for almost a year, and she thought he understood her, but apparently he never really tried. Maybe that was her problem. Did she expect men to dive deeper when all they were really capable of was skimming the surface?

"Won't know just how easy it'd be to fall under my spell until you try..." Mace countered, his teasing suggestion drawing her out of her reverie.

His skill in turning even the most mundane conversation into a flirtation made her laugh. "Why do I feel like the hare to your rabbit? I'm here for a week, Mace. Think marathon, not sprint."

2

"Sure you don't want me to help you with that?" Mace drawled from his leaning position against the stable door.

Sabrina tossed her long dark braid over her shoulder and blew wispy bangs away from her eyes to look at him. "I know exactly what you want to help me with, Mace Tanner, and the only one getting a rubdown is Lightning." She smirked, then turned back to the horse to unbuckle the saddle.

"I'm good with my hands. It's been a few days now. How long you gonna keep me at bay, darlin'?"

"'Til the cows come home."

After several seconds of total silence, the sound of a cowbell ringing and mock mooing coming from the stall doorway had her laughing out loud. Pulling the saddle off the horse, she put it away and called over her shoulder, "Go back to work, Mace. I'll join you for dinner later."

"You know you're breakin' my heart, don't ya?"

When Sabrina cut her gaze back to Mace, he had a cowbell

hanging from his neck and his hand over his heart. The expression on his face reflected sheer pain.

She snorted. "The only thing I'm breaking is your string of successful seductions."

Elise's laughter floated from behind Mace before she appeared beside him. Looping her arm around her brother-in-law's, she bumped shoulders with him. "She's got ya there. Come on, Mace. You've played constant host since Bri arrived. Let's give her a few moments alone." She locked gazes with Sabrina and rolled her eyes. "Even if she wants to spend them working."

Sabrina shrugged. "The horses enjoy it...and it relaxes me, strange as that sounds. See you guys in a half hour," she called after them as Elise pulled Mace away.

Turning back to Lightning, Sabrina looked around for the grooming brush until she spotted it up on a wood shelf on the wall. "Didn't these Tanner men realize that not everyone in this world was over six feet tall?" she muttered to herself as she stood on tiptoe to try to reach the horse brush from the high shelf. Not quite tall enough.

She lowered her arm and looked around the horse's stall. No stepstool in sight. Sighing, she stood on her toes again, straining her calf muscles. Her fingers brushed the bristles, then pushed the brush back away from the edge of the shelf.

Great. Now she couldn't even see it.

Lightning neighed, apparently impatient for her to get on with the grooming part. After being on the ranch for three days, Sabrina still hadn't gotten up the nerve to ride a horse by herself, but she'd asked Elise to show her how to groom one. Turns out she really enjoyed the task. It was like pet therapy or something.

Eventually she'd work her way up to riding a horse on her own, but in the meantime, she convinced Elise to let her give Lightning a good rubdown when her friend arrived back from rides with Colt.

Mace had been a gracious host and constant companion, all the while never giving up on seducing her. And as much as she had fun joining in their outrageous flirtation, she didn't let it go any further.

She liked Mace, found him very attractive, but she held back, not really sure why. She didn't feel guilty not indulging with Mace, because the only rule she'd planned to follow while here was; "if he trips your trigger, go for it". Mace made her laugh and her ego soar, and she could see how he'd trip many women's triggers, but she just wasn't one of them. She had to give the man an "A" for effort though. Sabrina snickered as she put one hand against the wall while reaching up in one last attempt to retrieve the grooming brush.

"Here, let me help ya." Strong hands came around her waist at the same time a hard chest pressed against her back, causing her to freeze and her heart race. He smelled so good, like faint cologne and leather. God, he smelled of *leather*, she thought as he easily lifted her so she could retrieve the brush. Sabrina quickly grabbed the brush and waited for the man to set her down so she could see his face.

Instead, he lowered her slowly to the ground, his voice's deep timbre skidding down her spine, "I don't think I'd ever be allowed on this property again..." He paused and let go of her waist to push her heavy braid away from her neck, then whispered in her ear, "If Colt knew the impure thoughts running through my head right now."

Sabrina's heart slammed as heat rushed to every part of her

body. She couldn't believe her reaction to this man she'd yet to see, but who obviously mistook her for someone else.

She started to speak when the stranger set her away, saying in a gruff tone, "I'm sorry, Elise. I shouldn't have said that."

Sabrina turned around, eyebrow raised. "Then, I guess it's a good thing I'm not Elise, so those impure thoughts can just stay between you and me."

He quickly swiped his straw cowboy hat off his head and an embarrassed expression crossed his face. "I'm sorry, ma'am. Please forgive me."

"No worries. I've been mistaken for Elise before." She scanned the man's six-foot-tall form, and the first thing that came to mind would definitely fall in the impure thoughts category. Trim, jean-clad hips, a silver and gold buckle, a black T-shirt that fit his muscular physique very well, broad shoulders, and the sexiest, square jaw she'd ever seen. She usually preferred clean cut and custom suits to overnight scruff and Wranglers, but the intense look in his arresting teal green eyes before he realized she wasn't Elise was what ultimately snagged her attention. She'd love to have a man look at her like that. He had the sexiest wavy blond hair she'd ever seen. It was an appealing just-rolled-out-of-bed look that made her want to touch it. "And as for impure thoughts...they're only bad if they aren't returned," she finished," she said, flashing a grin.

His regretful look changed to surprise, and then a broad smile spread across his face. Placing his hat on his head, he held out his hand. "I'm Josh Kelly. My family owns the neighboring Double K ranch."

Sabrina shook his hand. "Nice to meet you, Josh. I'm Sabrina Gentry, a college friend of Elise's visiting for a bit."

Josh's grip was firm, and once he shook her hand, he didn't let go. "Are you from Virginia too?"

She looked down at their clasped hands, mesmerized by his warmth and the tingling sensation sliding up her arm. Blinking to clear her head, she met his gaze. "No, I live in Arizona."

"Ah, so you're used to the heat, then."

His Texas drawl, coupled with his arresting gaze lingering on her lips, made her stomach dip. *Was it getting hot in here?* She let go of his hand and turned to begin brushing Lightning. "Yes, I'm very used to the heat."

Josh's hand landed on hers and he spoke next to her ear. "Here, this is how you do it," Slowing her movements, he guided her hand across the horse's back, showing her the best way to stroke the hair.

His cologne tickled her nose as he demonstrated his technique. When his chest brushed against her back, she resisted the urge to lean against him, but she couldn't help closing her eyes and inhaling his arousing, masculine scent.

"See," he said, his voice soothing and calm as Lightning pawed the ground. "She likes slow but firm strokes."

Sabrina's body instinctively migrated closer to him, her arm moving fluidly with his. She liked a man who took the time to understand what a woman wanted, even the animal kind. That just meant he'd be even better with the human version.

Lightning neighed again and turned her head, causing Sabrina to open her eyes. When she saw Josh put his hand out and the horse turn to rub her nose in his palm, she chuckled. "You sure have a way with women, Josh Kelly."

"I try my best to please." He spoke close to her ear, the deep baritone sliding across her skin like an invisible caress.

"I'll just bet you do. How sorry were you that Colt snagged Elise?" she asked as he let go of her hand and moved to stand in front of Lightning to rub the horse's nose.

Josh shot a grin her way. "Elise who?"

"Well, aren't you quick on your feet." She laughed, appreciating his wit.

"Josh?" Elise called as she rounded the corner to enter the stall. "There you are. I saw your horse and wondered where you went off to."

"Hey, Elise. I came looking for you and ran into Sabrina."

Sabrina watched Josh's reaction to Elise with interest. His relaxed stance had changed to an alert one the moment she entered the stables.

"Thanks for coming," her friend replied. "You ready for the kids?"

A half-smile tugged at his lips as he rubbed the back of his neck. "The Lonestar's a hard act to follow, but we're working on an activity I think the kids will love."

"That's great," Elise said, beaming. "They were so excited when I told them your ranch was their camp's next stop."

"We'll be ready for them. You ah, mentioned a bull in your voicemail."

Elise nodded. "We're hoping to trade it for another horse, like Colt did with Lightning. Are you interested in taking a look?"

"Yeah."

"Lightning was your horse?" Sabrina turned a narrowed gaze toward Josh. He'd led her to believe Lightning had taken to him so quickly.

Josh winked and tapped his fingers over his heart. "She misses me sorely."

"Yep, Lightning was Josh's horse." Elise gestured to the horse. "Colt traded a bull for her as a gift to me."

"He one-upped me on that one." Josh's lip curled in annoyance.

"You got the bull you wanted," Elise said, grinning.

Sabrina saw the look on Josh's face when Elise teased him about the bull, and her attention pinged to Elise for any recognition of his affection. *That's not the only thing he wanted, Elise.*

"Come on." Elise beckoned Josh. "I'll show you our bull." Pausing, she turned to Sabrina. "Hurry up, slowpoke. Dinner's almost ready. Nan's cooking a special meal tonight for our guest."

Sabrina shot her a pleased look. "Just for me?"

"Of course you, silly. So get a move on and head over to the kitchen. Nan likes company while she's cooking. I'll meet you there once I finish up with Josh."

Josh turned to her and pulled on the front of his hat. "Nice to meet you, Sabrina. Hopefully I'll see you again."

There he went again with that sexy drawl. It's like he knew the sound melted her from the inside out. *You can bet on it.* She smiled. "Nice to meet you, too. I'm sure I'll see you around." *Even if I have to show up on your doorstep, Mr. Hunky Neighbor.*

Once Elise and Josh walked off, Sabrina finished up with Lightning, then made her way over to the kitchen.

"Hi, Sabrina," the older lady called out from her position near the stove. Her white teeth made a striking contrast against her dark skin as she gave Sabrina a broad, friendly smile. "Come on in and sit down. Tell me how you're enjoying your vacation so far."

"Oh, no, you don't. I might be a guest, but I like to do my fair share." Sabrina approached the sink and washed her hands. "How can I help?"

"I like you." Nan beamed, gripping the skillet's handle to turn over a piece of chicken. Nodding toward the cooked potatoes in a blue and white bowl near the sink, she said, "Why don't you mash those up and then add some butter, milk, and salt and pepper."

"Will do." Sabrina picked up the bowl and used the utensil Nan had sitting in it. While she mashed the potatoes, voices outside drew her gaze to the open window.

Elise and Josh stood talking outside. When Elise looked away, gesturing toward the pasture, Josh's gaze never left her friend's profile. He smiled, his expression intent as he listened. Yep, he definitely still had feelings for Elise. The knowledge made her a little sad for Josh. To want what you can't have was very unfulfilling. Sabrina found herself suddenly smiling when Josh laughed at something Elise said. She'd seen his wit first hand in the barn. Did he laugh easily? Did he have a serious side? She wanted to know more.

As he spoke, Josh glanced up briefly and his gaze locked with hers through the window. Her heart thumped when he nodded once, then shifted his attention back to Elise. What the gorgeous cowboy needed was a new distraction...and Sabrina was more than happy to fill the role.

Dinner with Mace, Colt, Elise, and Nan was a treat. Her first night at the ranch, Sabrina and Elise had gone out to eat, and the other nights had been Colt, Elise and her eating together. Mace had joined them once before, but tonight they all enjoyed a special home-cooked meal with Nan, making it extra special.

At the end of the meal, Colt had turned quiet as he picked up Elise's hand and kissed the palm. "The next two weeks won't go by fast enough," he said, his gaze earnest and totally engrossed in his wife.

Elise smiled and leaned in to kiss him on the cheek. "They'll go by faster than you expect, I imagine, since you'll be so busy following the rodeo to a few towns."

"Yeah, but you've *got* a distraction," he complained with a half-smile, nodding to Sabrina.

"Oooh, to have a handsome man say I'm a distraction and really mean it." Sabrina fluttered her lashes wistfully and fanned her face.

"Elise, have you noticed what a smokin' *distraction* your friend is?" Mace said, eyebrows raised suggestively. "I'm not getting a lick of work done."

Sabrina giggled and threw her uneaten biscuit at him. God, he was great for the ego, not to mention a lot of fun.

Just as a round of laughter spread around the table, the phone rang. Elise got up to answer it while Colt pinned a stern look on Mace. "You'd better learn to focus real quick, little brother. You're running the ranch while I'm gone."

"Ah, man, do I have ta?" Mace mock complained. He gave Sabrina a heated look. "I planned to play chase."

Sabrina's eyes widened. "You mean that's not what you have *been* doing since I got here?"

"Nah, darlin'. That was just warming up." He pushed back from the table and began to re-tuck his denim shirt into his Wranglers as if trying to look good for a date. "I might have to be the responsible one while Colt's gone, but I'll still have my nights free. Wanna go out with me tomorrow to Rockin' Joe's?"

"You really are a piece of work," Sabrina said, shaking her head.

"Don't encourage him. It'll be like a match to kindling," Colt warned in a dry tone.

Elise hung up, then picked up her plate and Colt's. "That was Josh. He has a few ideas for a new horse, but he's going to come by tomorrow to look over the horses we already have. He wants to suggest the right one to mix in with the group." She glanced Nan's way and nodded toward the doorway. "Go on into the living room with the guys and relax. Sabrina will help me with the dishes. Thank you for another wonderful meal."

"But she's the guest," Nan said, eyebrows lifted in surprise.

"Who's very grateful to be here and will happily do her part." Sabrina stood and shooed them on. "Now go take a break."

Nan grinned. "It's always nice to see the boys at the table." She cut her gaze between the two men and finished in an admonishing tone, "It doesn't happen near often enough. Colt, you be sure to tell Cade I expect him to visit soon."

"Will do, Nan. Hmmm, I believe we're being asked to make up for quality time. What do you think, Mace?"

Mace stood. "Guess we're breaking out the Scrabble board. I don't believe Nan's delivered her special dose of whoopass on us in quite a while."

Nan gave a deep belly laugh, her large breasts bouncing

against her full–figured frame. "Come on, boys. Let the *master* show you how it's done."

Elise smiled after the men and Nan as she began to scrape off the leftover food from the plates into the trashcan.

"They're very close, aren't they?" Sabrina opened the dishwasher and began to rinse the dirty dishes Elise handed her.

"Yes, Nan helped raise Colt and his brothers when his mother left."

"Ah, now I get it." Sabrina nodded her understanding at the family-like atmosphere she'd seen between Nan and the men.

They worked in silence for a while until all the dishes were done. While Elise was making a fresh pot of coffee, Sabrina dried her hands on a towel and leaned against the counter. "Want to hear my new philosophy on relationships?"

Elise poured the water in the coffee machine, then chuckled as she slid the pot in its holder and turned it on. "Knowing how picky you were about the men you dated in college, this should be interesting." Pulling a chair out she sat, green eyes alight. "Have a seat and spill."

"Picky? I just had standards," Sabrina began, then gave a wry smile. "Apparently I don't know jack. Before we broke up, Jeremy said I was too controlling. So here's the deal I made with myself. For the entire summer, I've decided to disregard my usual reservations concerning men and 'let myself go' with the first man who trips my trigger. I won't look too deeply or scrutinize, which is all I'll expect in return. I'm just going to live in the moment."

"Ah, now I know why you came to Texas. Appealing men abound." Elise nodded, then winked. "Fair warning, Bri, cowboys are an especially irresistible breed."

Sabrina shrugged, then brushed her long braid over her shoulder. "I'm not looking for Mr. Right to come from this adventure, but I made a promise to myself to not get caught in my normal hang-ups and I'm determined to stick with this plan. If nothing else, at least I can scratch this experience off my bucket list."

"Look out Texas men!" Elise leaned in to whisper, "Is Mace your 'project'?"

Sabrina shook her head. "I *love* flirting with that man, but as good-looking as he is, he doesn't do it for me like your neighbor Josh Kelly does." Sabrina held her breath and waited to see what kind of reaction she'd get from Elise.

Elise's eyebrows shot up, but then her expression turned serious. "Josh is a great guy, and yes, he's very nice on the eyes—"

"Why do I hear a *but* coming? Is he a womanizer or something—" Sabrina paused and quickly shook her head. "No, wait. I'm not supposed to ask."

Colt's phone started to ring, distracting them. Colt walked into the kitchen and swiped it from the counter.

Elise shook her head. "He's not a womanizer that I know of. That's not it—"

"I know Josh has a thing for you, Elise," Sabrina said in a lowered voice once Colt walked into the hall to talk. "I've seen the way he looks at you. If my interest in him makes you uncomfortable, I'll forget about it."

Her friend put a hand on her arm. "No worries, Sabrina. And yes there was a bit of rivalry between Josh and Colt, but that's in the past. It's just that—"

"Elise, it's your mom." Colt approached from the doorway,

phone in hand, a curious look on his face. "She couldn't get you on your cell, so she called mine."

"Excuse me for a second." Elise took the phone from her husband. "Hey, Mom," she said, then her face quickly pinched in concern. "Is he all right?" Colt put his hands on his wife's shoulders and pulled her close, mouthing, "Your father?" When Elise nodded, he massaged her shoulders, giving her his support.

Sabrina's stomach tumbled as her friend's face grew pale. *What's wrong? Not her dad too!*

"When's the surgery? I'll be on the next plane out. I know he doesn't want me to worry, but I want to be there when he wakes up." Elise's voice broke when she finished, "Mom, just in case...tell Dad I love him."

Tears fell once she ended the call. Colt turned her around and pulled her close. Kissing her forehead, he said, "I'm going with you, darlin'."

"But you can't go," she said between sniffles. "You've got all your travel plans made."

Colt shook his head. "Mace can go in my place. You're not going home alone. Just in case, I want to be there with you."

Elise hugged his waist and pressed a kiss to his jaw. "This is why I love you so much, Colt Tanner."

Sabrina's heart swelled for her friend and the obvious love she and her husband shared. She stood up from the table when Elise let go of Colt and walked over to her, a worried look on her face. "My dad had some heart pains and when he went to his doctor, they wouldn't let him leave for fear he'd have a heart attack. He's on the verge of one with clogged arteries. They've scheduled an emergency angioplasty tomorrow."

Sabrina's eyes teared. "Oh, Elise. I'm so sorry. I hope the surgery goes well. I'll leave first thing tomorrow morning."

Elise reached for her hand and shook her head. "Absolutely not! I'm only going to be gone for a couple of days. My dad's as tough as nails. He'll love the fact I'm there, but I'll be ready to come back once I know he's out of the woods."

"Are you sure?" Sabrina didn't want her friend to feel the need to accommodate her.

Elise squeezed her fingers. "Very much so."

While Colt called to make flight reservations, Sabrina asked in a low voice, "You started to say something about Josh..."

"Yes, I did..." Elise began, then paused. Holding Sabrina's gaze for a second, she pulled her into a hug and whispered in her ear, "Go for it, Bri. Grab life by the horns. You never know when you're going to get thrown, so you may as well savor the ride while it lasts."

Sabrina knew Elise was thinking about her father. She whispered back, "Your dad's going to be fine. I know it."

"I know he will." Elise clasped her tight, then leaned away and smiled. "I'm sure Josh would be happy to keep you company while I'm gone. I'll call him in the morning before I leave and tell him we'll have to hold off on the horse trade until I get back. Then I'll casually mention, 'But I do have a houseguest who might be bored out of her mind while I'm gone...'"

Sabrina grimaced. "Um, I'd prefer not to be so blatant."

"And acting on your 'trigger tripping theory' isn't?" Elise snickered at Sabrina's sour look before she moved over to the cabinets to retrieve some mugs. Glancing back at her, Elise sobered. "You changed after your dad died, Bri. Became more...contained over time. I'm glad to see you trying to open yourself up to possibilities." Turning to lean against the counter, Elise continued, "How about this...since Josh is supposed to come by tomorrow, I just won't let him know that I'll be gone. When he arrives, you can explain the situation? That work better for you?"

Sabrina grinned. "Much. What time was he supposed to stop by?"

"He just said late afternoon." Elise poured coffee into a cup. "That should give you plenty of time to dress to impress. I'm assuming that's your plan."

Batting her eyelashes, Sabrina adopted an innocent expression. "Whyever would you think that?"

3

"Stood up before we ever got started. This is a new low," Sabrina grumbled and looked at her watch. *Go figure I'd pick a man who can't even show up on time on the very first date. Trigger-tripping only works if he's around to make it happen.* The Texas sun beat down on her, its heat making her skin sticky and wet. She must've uncrossed and re-crossed her legs for the hundredth time while she sat on the front porch steps. Leaning against the railing, she hoped she appeared to be just resting and not the wilted flower she felt like.

Granted, Josh didn't know it was their first date or that she'd spent three hours getting ready, from deciding what to wear to her hair. *Three hours!* But he had made plans to meet Elise. It was six o'clock and the man still hadn't shown. Remembering she'd heard the phone ring not too long ago, she stood and walked inside, then veered into the kitchen, where Nan sat reading the paper. "Was that Josh who called?"

Nan lowered the newspaper and shook her head. "No,

hon, that was my sister confirming our dinner plans." Her brown eyes held an apology. "I feel bad leaving you, but we're celebrating her sixtieth birthday. Oh, speaking of which, let me get you a key to the house. There's an extra one in Colt's office." She started to get up, but Sabrina shooed her back in her seat. "Let me get it. I'm antsy. Where in Colt's office?"

Nan nodded. "It's in the top desk drawer. You can't miss it. It has the Lonestar brand on the key ring."

"Got it." Sabrina headed for the office near the living room. Just as she pulled open the desk drawer, a knock sounded at the kitchen door.

Someone rasped through the screen. "Where's Colt?"

Nan moved to the door. "He's not here and won't be back for a couple of days. What do you need, Jackson?"

Sabrina paused and listened, surprised to hear Nan sound less than friendly.

Coughing and hacking, the man said, "Tell Colt that if he can't keep his cows off my land, they'll become my property."

"You should quit smoking," Nan admonished. "Are you saying one of the fences is down?"

"Why else would I be here? Tell him to get the damned thing fixed. Now!"

Nan sighed. "Go home. We'll get the fence fixed."

After the man left, Sabrina grabbed the Lonestar key ring and walked into the kitchen. Nan was on the phone with someone, probably Colt's foreman. "Yeah, he said it's down and is being crankier than his usual self about it. Can you get it taken care of? Great. I'll be sure to let Colt know."

Once Nan hung up, Sabrina asked, "Who was at the door? He didn't sound too happy."

Nan rolled her eyes as she slid her oversized purse onto her shoulder. "That man's never happy. He's just an annoying neighbor."

Sabrina lifted the key ring. "Found it."

"Good. Well, guess I'd better get going."

Sabrina followed Nan outside.

"I'm sure it seems quiet around here without Mace," Nan said, glancing her way.

"Mace does have a certain addicting charm." Sabrina smiled. "I definitely miss his banter."

"That's our Mace. He always knows just what to say to the ladies."

"He's got it down to a science," Sabrina agreed.

Nan paused on the porch, looking reluctant to leave. "You're welcome to come with me if you'd like."

Sabrina patted her shoulder. "Go enjoy yourself. Don't worry about me."

Nan walked down the steps, then nodded toward the screen door once she reached the ground. "I left you a dinner plate in the fridge. You'll just have to heat it up when you're ready."

"Thank you, Nan. Go have a blast with your sister. You only turn sixty once."

"I've turned sixty for the past five years." Nan winked, a wide grin spreading across her face. "It's called 'sixty and holdin'.'"

Once Nan drove off, Sabrina decided she'd give Josh another half hour and sat down on the stairs once more. The wind kicked up, blowing her long hair away from her neck and giving her a break from the oppressive heat. That was another reason she was so hot. She'd left her hair unbound. She frowned at the crumpled wrinkles creasing her cream linen miniskirt and baby pink linen top.

The wind buffeted around her again, announcing evening's arrival. Sabrina glanced up to see dark clouds rolling across the night sky. Guess she'd better eat some dinner. Just as she shut the screen door behind her, the wind howled, causing the screen door to swing wide open and slam against the door jamb. The loud sound made her heart jerk. Holding her hand over her chest, she latched the screen and decided it was probably best to close the main door too.

While the smell of fried chicken and baked beans wafted from the microwave, Sabrina watched the wind bend the trees back and forth through the kitchen window, her fingers thrumming on the counter. *Why hadn't Josh shown up or at least called?*

She flipped on the TV, then sat down on the couch to eat. The television show's noise in the background made her feel less alone. Nan was right. She did miss Mace and everyone else. The house seemed so quiet now that they were all gone. When she thought of the reason for Elise's absence, Sabrina said a little prayer for her friend's father before she began to eat her meal. She hoped he made it through his surgery without any complications.

A warning flashed up on the TV screen, making her turn up the volume.

Earlier today, Eddie Clayton, convicted for the murder of his longtime live-in girlfriend, escaped the bus that was transferring him from his temporary cell to his permanent twenty-year stay in the state penitentiary. If you see this man, don't go near him, please call 911. He was last seen heading south on foot, where he disappeared into a stretch of woods off Highway 17.

The mug shot picture that flashed up on the screen of a menacing man with long black hair, a full beard and beady black eyes made her shiver. Wasn't Highway 17 only a few miles from the Lonestar ranch? "What part of Highway 17?" she asked the unresponsive TV. When the news flash ended, she clicked off the TV, regretting watching it. Now she'd be all jumpy, noticing every shadow.

Sabrina finished cleaning her dishes and turned off the light in the kitchen. Remembering her glass of water, she walked back into the dark room and swiped it off the counter. Something outside drew her attention. It sounded like a door had closed. She stared out the kitchen window. Then blinked when a light flashed in the darkness.

Her stomach tensing, she waited and stared in the direction where she thought she'd seen it. A light flickered again, making her heart leap. It was coming from the stables.

Had Josh shown up late and was checking out the horses himself before coming to the door? Why didn't he turn on the lights?

Could it be someone else? She recalled the news on the TV and a shiver of apprehension zipped along her spine. As her body tensed, it occurred to her that she had trouble with the main light switch in the stables cutting in and out while she was in there the other night. It had to be Josh!

As soon as she walked outside, Sabrina paused when she saw an oil lantern sitting on the porch railing. A piece of paper fluttered underneath it. She slipped the paper out from underneath the lantern.

Elise,

Meet me in the stables. I've got a couple things to go over with you.

Smiling, Sabrina set down the note and lifted the lantern, then carefully walked down the stairs in her heeled sandals. She was glad for Josh's company. That news flash had really spooked her.

She didn't let the buffeting wind or the rolling thunder announcing an impending storm bother her. She just wanted to see Josh again. Her steps briefly slowed. *What if he was disappointed that Elise wasn't meeting him about the horse?* Even as the worry entered her head, her heart still raced in anticipation of seeing him again. Hopefully her appearance in the stables would make him glad he came by anyway.

The wind had apparently blown the large stable doors closed. She had to pull hard to open one of the wood panels. Once she'd opened it enough for her body to squeeze through, she slid inside.

As the door slammed closed behind her, a couple of horses neighed, drawing her attention. She tried to ignore her heels sinking into the dirt floor as she turned the lantern light in their direction and shushed the agitated horses. Once they calmed a little, she called out in a hushed voice, "Josh, are you there?" *Why the heck am I talking so low?*

Maybe it was because the lantern made shadows appear to move throughout the otherwise pitch-black stables, but the darkness, combined with the sound of the wind buffeting the stable walls outside, made knots form in her stomach. Not to mention, the idea of some psycho-killer running around not too far away didn't help either.

As she walked toward the horse's stall that was still making low agitated sounds, she realized Josh never answered her. "Josh Kelly, I'm spooked enough as it is tonight," she hissed out in a whisper once more. "I don't need you goofing around. You'd better show yourself or...I'm going to tell Colt what you said to me yesterday."

When Josh didn't acknowledge her, the knot in the pit of her stomach turned to queasiness. A cold feeling shot down her spine right before the hairs on her arms began to stand up. Something definitely didn't feel right. Sabrina turned, intending to retrace her steps out of the stables when a man spoke from behind her in a low voice, "Two birds."

Strange comment aside, the odd coldness in his tone made her bolt. Sabrina had only taken a couple of steps when a sharp pain lanced through the back of her skull.

Groggy, she fell to the dirt floor and thought she heard him whisper, "One stone."

Scents of earth, hay and horseflesh filled her senses as bits of hay dug into her cheek. Pain wracked her head and she tried to speak, but her voice refused to work.

As her vision started to blur in and out, Sabrina blinked to focus, but couldn't.

Then everything went black.

Sabrina woke feeling like someone had used her as a punching bag. She tried to turn her head in order to determine where she was, but pain ricocheted from the base of her skull, making her moan into the pillow.

She started to lift her hand to her head, but a sharp sting across the back of her hand caused her to gasp. Someone quickly leaned across her and grabbed the IV pole that had tilted with her swift movement, righting it.

"Hi there." Josh pushed her hair back from her eyes as he looked down at her, worry and relief flickering in his gaze. Dirt and hay clung to his light blue t-shirt, and he smelled of smoke. Black smudges streaked across his face.

"You look as bad as I feel," she croaked.

The corner of his mouth tilted and amusement crept into his eyes. "You must not be too bad off then, or do you always wake up handing out compliments?"

She managed a half-smile. "I'm not a morning person. That's for sure. Uh, is it morning?" she asked, confused.

"No, it's a quarter 'til midnight. But as far as your comment on not being a morning person," he paused and gently ran his thumb along her jaw. "I'll keep that in mind."

As a flush crept along her cheeks, she glanced around the sparse room for a distraction. A bed table, IV pole, gurney-style bed, and the unbecoming floral print gown wrapped around her pretty much clued her in. "Why am I in a hospital?"

Josh's brows drew together and he reached for her hand. "You don't remember what happened?"

Her heart thudded and her stomach tensed; how had she gotten there and why did her head hurt so damn bad? As she slowly shook her head, he cupped his fingers around hers. The gesture helped calm her frazzled nerves, sending a fuzzy feeling of comfort spreading through her.

"Why were you so late?" she asked, trying to remember when he finally showed up at Elise's house. Staring at his tousled blond hair and the appealing five o'clock shadow on his jaw, she wondered how she could've forgotten him finally showing up.

"I'd say he got there just in time." Nan's upbeat voice came from the other side of the bed as she approached from the open door. The older woman patted her other hand, then picked it up and squeezed. "I'm so thankful you're okay. I came back early to see Josh tugging on the stable doors. He ran in and horses scattered right before he carried you out. The chaos of smoke and fire trucks—"

"Stable? Smoke and fire trucks?" Sabrina's voice rose and her stomach dropped, her gaze pinging to Josh's. "What fire trucks?" A fire would definitely explain his smoky, sooted appearance.

"The stables were on fire while you were unconscious inside," he said, eyes searching hers.

"Josh saved your life, Sabrina," Nan said, patting her shoulder.

"Oh my God," Sabrina raised a trembling hand to her mouth, afraid to ask, but she needed to know. "Did all the horses make it out okay?"

"They're fine, dear. Don't you worry about them," Nan answered calmly.

"What *do* you remember?"

Sabrina felt the urgency in Josh's steady gaze. She closed her eyes and tried to recall, but after a few seconds blew out her frustration, unable to fill the empty hole of time. "I waited for you to come to...tell you that Elise had to go out of town suddenly." She rubbed her temple, hoping the action would help the rest come back to her.

Nan took her shaking hand and squeezed, concern on her lined face. "I know you're rattled. Take your time."

"All I remember was hearing a sound and peering outside to see what caused it. And...and..." Sabrina struggled, but it was a complete blank after that. Fear slammed into her and she started to breathe in and out in shallow breaths.

"Calm down. Deep breaths," Josh soothed. "You don't remember anything else?"

"I remember someone or something hitting me in the back of the head." She winced at the memory flash of pain, then frowned. "But you said I was in the stables? I don't remember going there. I don't remember how it happened. I...I just don't know."

"Inhale, Sabrina," he said calmly.

She inhaled to slow her breathing, then slowly shook her head. "No, I'm sorry. That's all I remember."

He sighed, then looked at Nan. "The doctor won't let her talk to the police until he's checked her out."

"The police?"

Josh nodded. "I stopped by to apologize to Elise for missing our appointment when I smelled smoke." He met her gaze, his expression serious. "The stables were on fire and someone had shoved a stick between the door handles, locking the building from the outside. Nan told you the rest. The doctor mentioned that you have a knot on your head—so that falls in line with what you've said about being hit from behind. We're not sure yet if the fire was intentional, but whoever hit you must've locked you in."

Glancing over to Nan, he said, "Would you mind getting the doc, then the police can talk to Sabrina."

Once Nan left to get the doctor, worry tightened Sabrina's chest. "None of this makes any sense. Why would anyone try to hurt me? No one knows me here."

"Maybe you were just in the wrong place at the wrong time." His eyes darkened, churning with unfathomable intensity. "Don't worry, Sabrina. I won't let anyone harm you."

She tilted her head and for a brief second enjoyed the feeling of being watched over. "Why can't I remember what happened during that pocket of time, yet I clearly remember what you said to me in the stall the day before when you thought I was Elise. I guess the fire doused your plans to meet with her." When she realized how that must've sounded, she quickly added, "About the horse, I mean." *Well, crap! Why does it bother me so much that he cares about Elise? I just met the man for Pete's sake!*

His eyes held hers for a long second, then he nodded. "I've heard being hit on the head can sometimes cause partial memory loss."

"Er, sorry. I didn't mean to imply...about Elise. It's just that—"

"I've obviously been on your mind?" he suggested, a cocky half-smile tugging at his lips.

"No, that's not what I meant—"

"I *was* the first thing you brought up."

Embarrassed heat rushed her cheeks. "No, seeing you brought it back. I mean—"

"About Elise...once upon a time, maybe." A serious look settled on his face as he clasped her hand and sat next to her. "But yesterday was the first time I've ever been attracted to Elise's backside."

He paused and ran the pad of his thumb along the inside of her palm, his intimate touch stealing the air from her lungs despite the dull pounding in her head. "If you had any idea what I thought about doing with you the rest of the day after I laid eyes on you, you wouldn't be questioning what woman I want to get to know on a personal level, 'cause I sure as hell don't."

His blunt confession skittered along her spine, while his electrifying touch made her heart skip several beats. Unsure how to respond without stammering even more, she was saved by Nan walking into the room accompanied by an older, silver-haired man with gold-rimmed glasses. Josh stood but stayed close as the doctor approached her bed.

He pulled his stethoscope out of his coat and smiled, his tone upbeat. "Hi there, young lady. I'm Amos Shelton. You gave us quite a scare tonight." Glancing at Josh, he said, "Stand back, please, and let me have a look at my patient."

When Josh moved away to allow him room to work, the doctor checked her out thoroughly. Once Dr. Shelton finished his exam, Josh asked him, "Is she up to going home tonight?"

The man looked thoughtful. "She doesn't appear to have a concussion. As long as she's going to have someone watch out for her for the next hour or so, then I'll release her."

The older man looked at her and asked, "There are police officers outside who want to ask you some questions. Are you feeling up to it? If not, I can tell them to call you tomorrow."

"I'm fine to answer questions," she said. The doctor nodded, then stepped into the hall and returned with two officers in tow.

"Hi, Miss Gentry," the male police officer with blond hair said as he entered the room and pulled out a pad and a pen. "I'm Tom Jenkins. He nodded to the redheaded woman next to him. "And this is my partner, Renee O'Hara. We're the investigating officers on this case. Are you feeling well enough to give us a statement?"

Sabrina ran through the exact same scenario she'd described to Josh and Nan.

"Are you sure there's nothing else you can remember?" the female police officer asked as she tucked a stray lock of hair that had escaped her ponytail behind her ear.

Sabrina started to shake her head, when she remembered something unusual. "I remember carrying a lantern, but," she paused and frowned, "I'm not sure why.

The woman looked at her partner. "It's possible you heard or saw something and went to investigate."

Sabrina raised her eyebrows. "What's weird is I couldn't tell you where to find a flashlight in Elise's house, let alone a lantern."

"There's an old lantern just inside the door of their stables," Josh supplied. When they all looked at him, he shrugged. "What? I'm observant."

Officer O'Hara cleared her throat. "Like I said, maybe you went to investigate and stumbled on the convict who recently escaped hiding in the stables. I heard he was picked up not more than two miles from the Lonestar. They're questioning him right now."

The idea that her assailant could've been a convicted murderer set Sabrina's heart racing. No matter who it was, someone had tried to hurt her. As a shiver passed through her, she managed to speak. "Thank goodness you caught him."

"We'll let you know once we hear back from the arresting officers if he admits to being on the Tanners' property," Renee said. "Just in case this man wasn't your attacker, it's probably best if you stay somewhere else for tonight."

She hadn't thought about going back to an empty house.

Even though Nan was there as early as six in the morning, she had her own place. "Oh, I guess I could check into a hotel—"

"She'll stay with me."

Sabrina turned a surprised look Josh's way. "Um..."

"Of course she'll come back with me," Nan interjected. "I'll stay at the Lonestar in the other guest bedroom."

"The doc says you need to be watched for a while longer." Josh held Sabrina's gaze, his jaw set at a stubborn angle. "I'm a night owl."

"I'm...I'm not sure." Sabrina's gaze pinged between Josh and Nan, feeling as if she was intruding on their lives.

"What are your wishes?" the doctor asked.

"She'll stay with the Kelly family," Josh insisted in a final tone. "I'll bring her back to the Lonestar tomorrow, Nan."

"Josh Kelly, I've never seen you be so demanding," Nan said, eyebrows raised.

"It's all right, Nan." Sabrina tried to smooth the obvious tension between them. "Josh earned the right to be a bit demanding tonight. I kind of don't want to go back to the Lonestar until morning if you don't mind."

When Nan nodded her understanding, the blond police officer asked Josh, "Have Colt and Elise been informed of the situation?"

"I left a message on Colt's cell for him to call me."

"Good." He closed his notepad and tucked it in his back pocket. "Let us know when you reach him."

"That's enough questions and people for now," the doctor said, ushering the police officers out of the room.

Once the physician closed the door, Nan pulled out a sealed plastic bag of biscuits from her oversized purse and whispered, "Are you hungry? Hospital food is never good."

Sabrina smiled when the doctor came back in the room and Nan quickly shoved the biscuits into her purse.

"Okay, Nan Marie." He rubbed his hands together. "Let's see what goodies you've got stowed away in that big purse of yours. Did you really think I couldn't smell your good cooking a mile away?"

Just as Nan grinned and retrieved the bag of food, the phone on the nightstand rang.

Josh answered. "Kelly here."

Sabrina tensed when Josh said, "Hey, Colt. She's a bit bumped and bruised, but the doc says she's fine. All the horses made it out okay. We've got them in our stables for now since yours are smoky and waterlogged. Yeah, I think once they dry out just one section will need to be repaired."

Josh met her gaze as he continued talking. "Someone knocked her out, then set the stables on fire. No, right now she doesn't remember what happened. The police think Sabrina might have surprised an escaped convict who may have been hiding out in the stables." Josh nodded and sat on the bed beside her once more. He rubbed his thumb across her palm in a slow, rhythmic motion, his gaze on hers. "Don't worry. I'll keep an eye on her until you and Elise get back."

Sabrina's heart raced while Josh continued to touch her hand as if it was the most natural thing for him to do. The intimate way he looked at her, as if they'd known each other for years, made a slow burn of awareness flutter through her. He distracted her so much she barely noticed her headache anymore.

Josh handed her the phone, drawing her out of her musings. "Elise wants to speak with you."

Sabrina took the phone. "Hello?"

"Oh my God, Bri, I can't believe this happened! Are you really all right?"

"I'm fine, Elise," Sabrina answered in a calm voice. "How's your dad?"

"There was a small complication after the surgery, so I won't be able to come home for a couple more days. I'm so sorry, Sabrina."

Sabrina heard the fear and regret in her friend's voice. She squeezed Josh's hand. "Don't worry. Josh promised to take good care of me."

"Oooh, he did, did he?" Elise's sudden interest overrode the worry in her voice. "Sounds like you've got him right where you want him."

Sabrina stared at Josh's hand on hers. "Close."

"I want to hear all about it when I get back," Elise insisted. "In the meantime, stick to Josh like glue."

Sabrina looked up at Josh's handsome face, felt the tender touch of his work-roughened hand on hers, the heat of his muscular thigh against her hip and smiled. "You don't have to tell me that twice. See you in a couple days." Hanging up, she asked, "When can we leave?"

4

The irony that she'd been saved from a fire when her father hadn't been so lucky didn't escape Sabrina. Instead of letting the tragic past replay in her head, she took a deep breath and focused on her rescuer as she rode beside him in his truck. Her head still felt tender, but at least it wasn't pounding any longer thanks to the painkiller the doctor had given her.

Josh pulled up to a large ranch house. Even though the lights were off, she could see its overall size in the starlit night. He quickly walked around to her side and opened the door for her. "We're here."

Clasping her hand, he helped her out of the truck. His cowboy hat hid his expression, but she could feel his intense stare. He didn't let go of her hand, but laced his fingers with hers and stepped so close his thighs brushed against hers.

He literally towered over her, his broad, muscular shoulders making her feel very petite standing in front of him. "Welcome to the Double K, Sabrina."

He spoke with such sincerity, his tone filled with pride, it was almost as if he were saying, "Welcome home." Regardless of how he meant it, that's how Sabrina took his sentiment. A feeling of comfort settled over her. Laying her free hand on his chest, she inhaled his smoky, masculine scent and breathed out, "Thank you for looking out for me."

He cupped her cheek, running his thumb along the edge of her jaw. "I'm just glad I got there when I did. I don't want to think about the alternative."

He stood so close he made every nerve in her body jump to attention. Sabrina tilted her chin higher and let out a nervous laugh. "You and me both. I kind of like living—"

Josh's lips touched hers, cutting her off. It was the barest brush, but Sabrina welcomed it. Breathing against his mouth, she pressed closer.

His hand traced to the back of her head and cupped it gently. Tilting her head, he murmured, "You taste even better than I imagined," right before he slid his tongue against hers in a slow, sensual glide, deepening their kiss.

Sabrina's heart thudded as his lips slanted over hers with an intensity she'd never felt with another man. The passion in his kiss lit her on fire, running to every nerve in her body in rushing, tingling waves.

She let out a pleased sigh against his mouth and gripped his waist, tugging on his t-shirt to pull him closer.

Josh's chest rumbled and one hand dipped to her back, arching her closer as he stepped into her. Just as he pressed her against the truck door, the porch lights came on behind them.

He broke their kiss and their heavy breathing comingled as he set his forehead against hers. "Damn, Brina."

From his heated, muscular body surrounding her to the sweet nickname he'd given her, he left her speechless and very glad she had the truck to lean on. She wasn't sure if she'd be able to stand on her own until the fluttering in her stomach settled. No man had ever made her feel this woozy with just a kiss.

A screen door squeaked open and Josh sighed. Curling his arm around her shoulders, he pulled her to his side and turned her toward the house.

An older woman wearing casual gray lounge pants and a matching top stepped outside. "Hey, Josh. Nan called and told me you'd be bringing Sabrina here. I've put her in your old room since the guest bedroom is in shambles with the remodel. Your room is next on the to-be-renovated list," she finished, grinning.

"It's about time you're finally getting around to my room, Mom. You're up really late." Walking toward the house with Sabrina, he continued, "I planned to take Sabrina on to my place. Was just stopping to get extra blankets."

"No, sir. Not tonight," his mother insisted while she stepped off the porch and approached them. Hooking her arm with Sabrina's, she pulled her out of Josh's embrace and gave her son a meaningful look. "You can sleep on the couch if you don't want to go on to your place."

"Hi, Sabrina," she said, smiling. "I'm Julia. Come with me, dear. I know you must be exhausted."

With Julia's expressive eyes and wavy, short blonde hair, Sabrina saw where Josh got his good looks. Her smile reminded Sabrina of Josh's too. As Julia led her away, she asked his mother, "Would it be possible for me to take a quick shower? I feel so grimy." She glanced past her dirt-smudged skirt and top that smelled strongly of smoke, to her muddy sandals and grimaced.

"Sure you can. I'll give you something to sleep in and a change of clothes to wear back to the Lonestar tomorrow. I'm so sorry what happened tonight. I'm just thankful Josh was there to save you," Julia rambled as she walked Sabrina into the house and steered her through the comfortable living room with beige and navy blue furniture and sky blue accents. Once they exited the living room, she turned down a hall.

Stopping at the last door on the right, she opened it, then looked over her shoulder at her son, who'd followed them. "Sabrina needs rest after what she's been through, Josh. Say good night while I get her some clothes and then it's off to the couch with you."

Sabrina watched his mother walk down the hall, her steps assured as she opened a door and disappeared into one of the bedrooms.

Despite how tired she felt, she met Josh's gaze and smiled. "Your mother's a lovely woman. I see you get your smile from her."

Josh leaned his forearm on the doorjamb and used his thumb to push back the brim of his hat. "Why, thank you, ma'am." Purposefully drawing out his Texan drawl, he grinned wider.

Sabrina's pulse raced when he leaned close and his five o'clock shadow brushed against her cheek. "Sweet dreams, Brina."

As she watched him walk down the hall, low slung jeans formed perfectly to his nice ass, her stomach flip-flopped. Instead of following him down the hall like she wanted to, she forced herself to walk into the bedroom and wait for his mother.

Julia returned within a minute, handing her towels, soap, shampoo, and a hairdryer along with a pair of jeans, some tennis shoes, and a white button down shirt for the next day. She'd also included a lavender ankle-length, cotton nightgown that buttoned all the way up the neck.

Sabrina suppressed her amusement over the *prim* nightgown and gave Josh's mother a smile of thanks before she headed for the bathroom.

After she finished showering and drying her hair, she looked around Josh's childhood room for a few minutes. Sports trophies lined the desk and certificates of achievement in athletics and academics covered the walls.

The revolver lying in front of the mirror on his dresser drew her attention. She ran her finger along the thick coating of dust covering the Colt 45's handle. Dust embedded in initials that had been etched in the metal. She bent close and read JK. Why was this vintage piece here instead of on display? she wondered as her gaze slid to the picture on the mirror.

Tucked in the corner of the mirror, the picture was of a young blond-haired boy around seven or eight wearing fireman's gear. A boy with dark brown hair and wearing a police officer's uniform had his arm slung over the blond boy's shoulders. *Halloween costumes, perhaps?* Big grins lit their faces as they each held up a cardboard bullseye target riddled with holes.

The smile gave the blond kid away. It was Josh's smile.

When she turned to the twin bed, she noticed a man's white t-shirt neatly folded on the pillow that hadn't been there before. Picking it up, she put the material to her nose and inhaled. Josh must've left it for her while she showered.

The shirt smelled like him...well, the way he'd smelled yesterday when she'd met him in the stables. Had she really just met him for the first time thirty-six hours ago? Then again, tragedies had a way of steamrolling through the crap that usually takes weeks to bring people closer together.

Pulling off the nightgown Josh's mom had given her, she slipped into his t-shirt, which fell halfway to her knees, then turned off the light.

The house wasn't overly cool, so she folded the heavy quilted comforter to the bottom of the bed, then slid in between the cotton sheets.

As soon as she pressed into the pillow, her mind shifted back to Josh. Their first meeting wasn't the most common for two people to have, nor was their second for that matter, she thought, a wry smile tugging on her lips. No wonder it felt as if they'd known each other much longer. That had to explain the instant connection she felt whenever he was close.

She recalled the way his warm hand felt on hers, remembered his hard chest against her back as he'd helped her groom Lightning. Closing her eyes, she pictured his handsome face and sexy smile and imagined him pulling her close like he'd done a few minutes ago. How could a man who kissed like that still be single? *Stop thinking. No questions, Sabrina. Just enjoy the moment, remember?* Moments she could easily handle. She conjured the feeling of his lips on hers and let out a wistful sigh.

"I hope that sound is for me," came a man's whisper next to the bed.

Sabrina jerked up on her elbow, a startled gasp rushing forth.

"Shhh." Josh put his finger over her lips. "It's just me," he continued as he sat down next to her. "Everyone's in bed, but I promised I'd keep an eye on you for at least another half hour. And I always keep my promises."

The outside lights gave off some illumination in his room, allowing Sabrina to see the slow smile that spread across his face as his gaze roamed over her shoulders. He looked pleased that she'd put on his t-shirt.

He smelled like soap and deodorant. Guess he'd taken a shower too. Sabrina ate up every inch of his bare torso. Light blond hair sprinkled across his muscular chest veeing its way down to hard abs that disappeared into his jeans. Every sexy inch of him begged to be touched. He hadn't bothered to put on the belt he had on earlier, as if he'd gotten dressed fast. The thought made her tingle and her chest tighten. No man had ever looked so incredibly irresistible as Josh Kelly staring at her as if he wanted to devour her.

She smiled and slid over on the narrow bed to give him room. "Looks like there's only one place to sit."

Josh flashed a quick grin and sat on the bed beside her. As he leaned back, his broad shoulders crowded hers for space against the narrow headboard. He gave a low laugh and he lifted his arm over her shoulders, then pulled her into his arms. "Somehow this just seems the right way to end a day like today."

"I couldn't agree more." She sighed and snuggled against his bare chest, wrapping an arm around his trim waist.

"Do you have any family?" Josh asked quietly, his fingers twirling the ends of her hair.

She nodded against his shower-warmed skin and ran her finger over a muscle that ran along his hip. “I have two older brothers and my mom. My...my dad passed away.” She was glad she was able to get that out without dwelling on the subject.

“I’m sorry, Sabrina,” he commented in a genuine tone as he lifted the strand he played with to his nose.

“He died a long time ago.” She didn’t really want to talk about her dad. “Tell me about the boy who used to live in this room.” She wanted to learn about the man who’d saved her life and held her in his arms as if he’d known her forever.

She felt him shift under her cheek and realized he was looking at the wall of trophies and achievement awards she’d noticed earlier.

“He was a good kid with an older brother and hard-working parents. He was happy-go-lucky, but also the competitive type, hence the sports trophies.” Josh’s chest rose and fell, and she felt, rather than saw, his amused smile.

“You mean you never gave your parents a bit of trouble?” She glanced up at him, a doubtful eyebrow raised.

His chest rumbled. “I didn’t say that. My brother and I gave our parents hell growing up. I’m just highlighting the good parts.” He laced his fingers with the hand she’d laid on his chest, then ran his other hand down her spine, spreading his fingers along her hip. “How else am I going to impress you?”

Heat radiated from his hand and she laughed, loving his sense of humor. “How indeed?” She laid her head back on his chest and slid her thumb over his. “So tell me about you and the little boy in the picture on your dresser.”

Josh's entire body tensed and Sabrina instinctively knew she'd hit a nerve.

After a few seconds, he relaxed and his fingers began to slide through her hair rhythmically. "Nick Austin was my best friend growing up. We got into all kinds of trouble as kids. Guess you could say he was the instigator, though I owned my part. Who knows how much more mischief we'd have gotten into if...well, he's gone now..."

Before he trailed off, she heard a hitch in his voice like it was too painful to talk about his friend.

Sabrina hugged his waist and whispered, "I'm sorry, Josh... for whatever happened."

He put his finger under her chin and lifted it. "I'd much rather focus on you." Their gazes met and he leaned close, his mouth a heartbeat away. "Ever since I held your sweet body against mine while you retrieved that damn brush..." he began, his gaze hungry and intense. "I'm sorry if I kissed you before you were ready. You just send me over, Brina."

"I remember being an active participant, so no apologies. Now, back to those impure thoughts you've been having..." she trailed off, letting her gaze drop to his mouth. If he didn't kiss her again, she'd kiss him. Her heart rammed as she waited for him to make the first move.

"Very impure thoughts."

The roughness in his voice made her really, really want to kiss him again, but her rational mind finally kicked in just before his lips touched hers. Placing a finger on his lips, she stopped him. If his mouth connected with hers, she wouldn't want to stop. For that matter, she'd kill him if he did stop. But tonight, in his parents' house, she needed to honor his mother's standards. "I want to kiss you very much, but we should respect your mother's home and her wishes."

Josh's gaze flared for a second before he playfully bit her finger. "You need your rest tonight anyway, but there's no reason I can't *tell* you what I'd like to do to you," he finished as he pulled her hand from his mouth and laid a warm kiss on her open palm.

The seductive look in his eyes told her this wasn't a good idea. In fact, it was probably the opposite of a good idea, but then she was already lying in bed with a guy she barely knew—who held and kissed her as if he'd known her forever. *Savor each moment, remember?*

He pressed his mouth to the heel of her hand, then moved his lips to the inside of her wrist, sending liquid heat flowing through her veins. Moving his lips along her arm, a low rumble sounded in his chest. "You smell so damn good. I want to taste you everywhere."

He met her gaze once more and continued with a heated look, "And I do mean *everywhere*."

Sabrina bit her lip to keep from telling him to start right this very second.

The corner of his mouth lifted in a sinful half-smile as he touched her nose. "I'd kiss you here." His finger traced to her lips. "And here—" Then he slowly drew a line down her throat and touched her rapid pulse. "I'd press my lips here to know how much you wanted me to continue branding the rest of your body."

Branding? Why did that sound so good to her? Sabrina's heart thudded and she began to throb as he hooked his finger along the top of the sheet, pulling it away. Ever so slowly, he ran his finger back up her stomach, then along the peak of a hard nipple. His t-shirt did nothing to muffle the stimulation.

"I'd tease this sweet peak with my mouth until I could see the pink color through the wet material. Then I'd nip at it just to hear you moan a little deeper."

The ache between her thighs beat in a pulse-like rhythm, following his verbal seduction and the lowering descent of his hand. So much tension was building inside her she unconsciously rubbed against him.

Josh took advantage of her movement and grasped her bare leg, pulling it over his until she was wrapped around his thick, hard thigh.

Sabrina sucked in her breath when he raised his leg slightly, purposefully pressing the hard length of his thigh intimately against her.

God, she'd never survive this. She closed her eyes and dug her fingers into his shoulders.

"I want to hear your breath hitch just like that when I touch you," he said, satisfaction lacing his tense tone.

He likes teasing me? Two can play at this game.

Sabrina ran her hand up his thigh and rested it on his hard erection through his jeans. She met his heated gaze when he hissed out a low groan. Using her other hand on the bed for leverage, she slid herself up the length of his body until her mouth hovered close to his. "Be careful, Josh Kelly. You might be the one to start this fire, but I promise I'll be the one to make it burn bright." As soon as she finished speaking, she squeezed him through the thick material and smirked when he inhaled sharply.

Josh slid his hands down her back and clasped her buttocks, his touch possessive as he pulled her fully on top of him. He didn't stop until they were as intimately connected as they could be with clothes on. The rough feel of his jeans through her thin silk underwear made it seem as if she were wearing nothing at all.

His eyes glittered in the darkness, full of challenge and desire as he pushed her hips down while he thrust upward, fitting himself inside her through their clothes, telling her exactly where he wanted to be.

"I know a good bit about putting out fires, Brina," he countered in a low, dark tone while his hands slid down to her rear to cup her buttocks once more. With a firm grip, he moved her just enough to rub her against the fly of his jeans.

Sabrina clasped his shoulders and bit her lip against the arousing friction. "Damn you," she hissed, then pounded one of his shoulders in sexual frustration.

"You're all fire...just like I thought you'd be," he said, a tight, satisfied smile tilting the corners of his lips.

His hands dropped to her bare thighs and he gripped the back of her legs, pulling her knees forward until she sat atop his hips.

She'd barely adjusted to the new position when he surprised her by swiftly changing positions until she was flat on the bed and he was leaning over her. Her breathing came out in short pants as he held her hands pinned to the bed above her head, his hips spreading her thighs, hard body pressing her against the soft mattress. Renewed arousal flared in his gaze. "I think you like me holding you down," he teased darkly.

When he didn't immediately release her, as if he were testing his theory, Sabrina tried to hide how much she enjoyed his dominance and began to tug in earnest to pull free. Josh's eyes glittered in the darkness and a pleased smile tilted his lips.

"You can release me now," she said, forcing a steady voice even as her chest thumped in excitement.

Josh's fingers loosened slightly as his gaze slowly traced her features. "It's a bit ironic that the woman who could've easily starred in every single adolescent wet dream I ever had will be sleeping in my childhood bed tonight."

His compliment shot straight to her belly and she breathed out, "Ironic?"

He leaned close, his breath warm on her cheek as he finished huskily, "Hell yeah, because I'll be on that couch dreaming of all the adult ways I *will* have you."

Before she could respond, he stood and scooped her in his arms. Settling her back on the pillow, he pulled the sheet over her and said in a controlled tone, "Good night, Sabrina. I'll see you in the morning."

Sabrina watched him leave the room, her body aching and throbbing for fulfillment. The promise in his words, the steady regard in his gaze when he told her they would be together echoed in her head, making her heart beat rapidly in anticipation. She'd never been more aroused and sexually frustrated in her life.

Yet she craved the anticipation too.

She wanted the attraction and tension build, let it simmer and burn. The way they'd ignited after just one kiss, she knew that when they finally came together, the explosion would be well worth the wait.

5

"Hi ya, girl," Sabrina crooned to Lightning over the stall door. "You'll be going home once the repairs are done." The horse snorted and pawed at the ground. Sabrina reached out and patted her nose. "But in the meantime, the Kellys will make you feel at home." When Lightning neighed and raised her head up and down as if in agreement, she couldn't help but smile. *Just like Josh's family had done for me this morning.*

After she'd gotten dressed and walked downstairs, she let her growling stomach lead her to the smell of bacon and eggs and coffee. The fact Josh wasn't present made her a little unsure what to do, but Julia met her in the living room with a sunny smile.

"Morning, Sabrina. Josh's up early, working on something or another. My son never lets himself relax. Come and eat. Everyone wants to meet you.

Josh never relaxes? He seemed pretty laidback to me.

"Everyone, meet Sabrina. Sabrina, meet the Kelly family,"

Julia said as they entered the kitchen and approached the table.

"Hi, I'm Ben," the blond-haired boy around ten piped up at the far end of the table. "If you're a friend of Josh's, you must be all right." His child's logic broke the ice and made her nervousness completely disappear as he rambled on, playing host. "That's my dad, Ben senior." He pointed to a tall, sandy blond-haired man pouring himself coffee by the sink. "And this is my mom, Lacey." He nodded to a woman with shoulder length auburn hair sitting next to him. "My grandpa—his name's Kenneth—is outside already since he's a real early riser."

"Good morning, Ben, and thank you for the welcome." Sabrina gave him an appreciative smile for the introductions before she sat down and enjoyed a wonderful breakfast with Josh's family. After breakfast, she'd wandered outside to check on the horses.

Where had Josh run off to? she wondered as she watched Ben and his father setting up bulls-eye signs at varied heights in what appeared to be some kind of elaborate target practice in the open pasture area next to the barn.

She'd just turned, intending to head back to the house to find Josh, when she saw him strolling her way, brown cowboy hat pulled low. Sabrina's mouth went dry as she watched him approach. Did he have any idea just how sexy he was in boots, low-slung jeans and a navy t-shirt that showed off the defined muscles in his arms?

When their gazes met and his lips crooked slightly, she inwardly sighed. Yeah, he knew. She suddenly felt incredibly dowdy wearing a pair of borrowed jeans two sizes too big. They were held up by a belt on its last loop and a plain white button down shirt tucked in the pants' waist to fill the gaps the belt couldn't. She hadn't bothered to put on the borrowed tennis shoes since they were a couple sizes too small. Great, that made her barefoot and dowdy.

"Good morning, beautiful," he said softly, his eyes crinkling in a smile.

"Morning, Josh. Do you always get up so early?"

"Yeah," he said, shrugging. "Lots of stuff to take care of." He nodded toward his brother and nephew. "Today's the Double K's turn to host the kid's camp."

"Oh yeah, I remember you and Elise talking about that," Sabrina said, trying to hide her disappointment that she wouldn't be spending the day with him. "Well, I'll get out of the way if you wouldn't mind taking me home."

He gave a decisive nod and folded his arms. "That's what I planned to do."

She swallowed the sudden knot in her throat, mad at herself for assuming he'd want to spend the day with her too, especially after last night. So much for *not* thinking ahead. Shifting her gaze to his boots so he wouldn't see the hurt in her eyes, she said, "Let me get my clothes and I'll meet you at your truck—"

"But Nan wouldn't let me."

Her gaze snapped to his. "Huh?"

Josh reached out and traced a finger along her jaw, sending goose bumps scattering along her arms. "I went to the Lonestar this morning to collect some of your clothes so you could stay with me," he began, then lowered his hand to his side and pressed his mouth in annoyance. "Nan refused to let me have anything of yours. Said she wanted to see for herself how you are doing. I've been ordered to bring you back to the Lonestar this morning."

His frown made her snicker. When it deepened, she sobered. "She's just looking out for me, Josh."

A serious look settled on his features. "That's my job."

Sabrina spread her hands and shrugged. "It's no one's job."

Josh's brow furrowed and he started to speak when Ben peered around the side of the barn, calling out, "Uncle Josh!"

"Yeah, Ben?"

Swiping sweaty bangs from his eyes, his nephew ran up. "Can you help us nail up the backboard Grampa built? Dad needs someone taller to help him hold it up while Grampa nails it to the stand."

Josh sighed and nodded. "Let me run Sabrina home, then I'll come help."

"You really like Josh, don't you?"

"Huh?" Sabrina peered over the clothesline as she straightened a bed sheet for Nan.

"You heard me." Nan set a couple of pins in place on the sheet, then lifted a fitted sheet and laid it across the line too.

"I like how he makes me feel." Sabrina moved to pull her freshly laundered clothes off the line. Just as Nan had promised, the warm Texas sun had done its job, drying her top and skirt in no time. And they smelled good too, like fresh outdoors.

As she folded her clothes, Nan stopped moving and pinned her with a look.

Sabrina shrugged. "What?"

"Aren't you going to elaborate?"

"Oh." Sabrina grinned. "Just special. Josh makes me feel special."

Nan nodded as she snapped some dry towels down from the line. "I'm glad to hear it. Josh is a good man. I like that he makes you smile."

Sabrina inwardly snickered at the tame term. If Nan knew her inner thoughts about Josh, she'd probably hose her down right in the yard. "Yes, he definitely makes me smile."

"I can tell. You haven't stopped grinning since Josh walked you to the door this morning."

Sabrina sighed as she recalled Josh's parting comment. The man knew just how to curl her toes.

He'd walked her all the way up to the door of the Lonestar, his warm hand resting at the base of her spine. "I'll be back to pick you up at three. Does that sound good? We'll go wherever you'd like."

She clutched her dirty bundle of clothes in her arms and turned to him. "Thank you for taking care of me last night, Josh. And I'd love to see your place." Tilting her head slightly, she grinned. "You know, a person's home can tell you a lot about him. What will yours tell me?"

He looked thoughtful as he pulled her close, wrapping his arms around her waist. "Probably that it misses me. I'm not there a lot."

Why wouldn't he be there much? Did he enjoy spending more time with his family at the Double K? Kind of like Elise and Colt do? Sabrina knew her friend and husband had their own house, but they'd stayed at the Lonestar the entire time she'd been visiting. The fact Josh enjoyed spending time with his family wasn't a bad thing.

He adopted an intrigued look and hooked his hands at the base of her spine. "What would I find at your place?"

She sighed wistfully. "Not you, unfortunately."

Josh flashed a pleased smile and his hold tightened. "I'll bet it smells just like you. All warm and sweet-smelling. Like a home should." He dipped his head and inhaled next to her neck before he brushed his lips against hers in a tender kiss. Stepping back, he touched the rim of his hat. "Then my place it is. Just you and me, getting back to nature."

Nan cleared her throat, bringing her to the present. The knowing look on Nan's face made Sabrina blush a little. Did she suspect more had gone on between Sabrina and Josh? Even though technically nothing had happened between them, the way Josh touched her and the things he'd alluded to doing with her last night definitely fell in the carnal category.

Sabrina pushed her loose braid over her shoulder and tried to sound casual. "I'm excited to see Josh again. He's coming to pick me up at three." *Why did I let Elise convince me to cancel my rental car? I could be there right now, helping with the camp.*

"So..." Nan began, tilting her head to the side. "I need to drive into town for some groceries soon. I could drop you off at the Double K around one. Would that make your smile turn megawatt bright?"

When Sabrina shot her a huge grin and started to quickly gather up her clean clothes, Nan laughed. "All I ask is that you bring Josh by the Lonestar for an early dinner tonight."

Sabrina's eyes widened as she crushed her clothes to her chest. "You knew I planned to stay the night?"

Nan snorted. "Sabrina girl, some things just shouldn't be

passed up. Josh is a handsome man and a good one too. If you weren't planning on it, I was going to pack your bag for you."

Sabrina snickered. "That's sounds exactly like something Elise would say."

Nan shot her a smug look. "Why do you think we get along so well?"

SABRINA HAD ASKED Nan to drop her off at the entrance to the Double K. She wanted to walk the half-mile distance along the drive to the ranch house, enjoying the view along the way. Just as she reached the end of the drive, gunshots filled the air. *Bam, bam, bam, bam, bam.*

Sabrina's heart raced as she tracked the noise near the barn. She let out a breath of relief when she saw Josh gesturing to the row of targets behind him. She'd assumed more than one person was shooting until she saw Josh holster his gun. Wow, had he fired all those rounds? She was pretty sure she'd heard five shots in under a second.

Josh stepped out of the way, then repositioned a teen boy in front of a target, which was a painted bulls-eye cardboard nailed to a post twenty five feet away. Once the kid lifted his gun, Josh straightened his elbow, positioned his shoulders, then gestured to the target for him to continue.

After she put her backpack on the front porch, Sabrina walked over to lean against the barn and watch Josh in action. He still hadn't noticed her, which suited her fine. She liked seeing him in his own environment, just being himself.

Five teens now stood lined in a row at their own target

stations. Each teen held an old-style six-shooter pistol at the ready.

When Josh stood off to the side and called out, "Go," they began firing, apparently competing to see who could hit his or her target with the most accuracy. Sabrina saw the bullets making holes in their targets but was surprised that they didn't make the same loud sounds Josh's gun had.

"Wax bullets," someone said from her right.

Sabrina nodded to acknowledge the woman with short dark hair. She looked to be in her late forties. "Ah, that makes sense for safety reasons." She shifted her gaze back to Josh and the gun belt hanging low on his waist. With his blue chambray shirt, cowboy hat and spurs on his boots, he could've been dropped into an old western film. Damn, he made a sexy cowboy.

"That old west look suits him," the woman commented, her gaze openly appreciating Josh's backside.

Well, who wouldn't? Sabrina thought even as a twinge of jealousy flared. "I was just thinking the same thing. I'm Sabrina."

"Name's Cynthia," she replied with a nod, her pale blue eyes now scanning the teens. "The Kellys really did a great job today; taught the kids how to saddle a horse and rope a calf too." She waved to Ben, who stood off to the side, ready to provide more ammo if needed, then nodded toward Josh. "Josh especially. He's so patient with them. These kids come from some pretty sad home situations. Between the Tanners' camp and the Kellys', I've never seen them smile so much."

The shooting stopped and Josh called out, "All right everyone, set your guns on your stations so I can check the results."

Sabrina could appreciate the kids' anticipation as she

watched him inspect each target. He finally pulled the one in the middle down and held it up, calling out, "Looks like Rebecca won."

The three boys and another girl congratulated the girl in blonde braids.

Josh grabbed the box that Ben handed him and approached Rebecca. "As the winner, you get a new hat," he said as he set a brand new beige cowboy hat decorated with a brown leather band on the girl's blonde head.

"Aw, man. If I'd have known there was a prize, I'd have tried harder," the boy to Rebecca's left said.

Josh grinned. "You all get a memento to take home." Pulling out a new horseshoe stamped with the Double K brand, he handed it to the boy, then walked down the line and gave each kid one.

Once he finished, he said, "Thank you for coming to the Double K. I hope ya'll enjoyed it."

The woman beside Sabrina approached the group, saying in a teacher's voice, "Okay, boys and girls. It's time to head for the bus. Thank Mr. Kelly and Ben here for hosting you."

Rebecca touched the top of her hat and grinned. "Goodbye, Mr. Kelly, thank you for everything."

"Thanks, dude," another boy with long bangs and a lip ring said in a subdued tone.

Once each kid had said their thanks and goodbyes, the group asked Ben to walk them to the bus.

The woman smiled after they walked away, then turned to Josh. "Thank you so much for doing this, Josh. It meant the world to them. I hope you'll consider doing it again next year."

Josh tugged on his hat. "My pleasure, Cynthia. And yeah,

we'll definitely offer this camp again next year. We had a blast."

As Cynthia walked past the barn and waved to Sabrina, Josh's gaze strayed to her leaning against the barn. A broad smile spread across his face. "How long have you been here? I thought I was coming to get you later."

"I've been here long enough to watch you in action. As for you coming to get me..." Sabrina approached, glad she'd dressed in jeans and an aqua blue short-sleeved button down shirt. She'd have been way overdressed in a skirt and heels. Stopping in front of him, she pushed her hands in her back pockets and rocked on her boot heels. "I thought I'd come to you."

Something flickered in Josh's gaze and he gently tugged on her braid lying across her shoulder. "I like the sound of that."

Heated tension settled between them, ramping her heart rate. Now that they were alone, nervousness began to flutter in her stomach. She gestured to the target area. "That was fun to watch. The kids really seemed to enjoy it." Glancing down at the gun on his hip, she continued, "My favorite part was seeing you dressed like an Old West gunslinger."

Josh followed her line of sight, then met her gaze, a playful look in his eyes. "Ever shot a Colt 45 before?"

She shook her head. "Never shot a gun in my life."

Grinning, he pointed to the middle wooden stand. "Then you're about to learn. Wait there."

While Sabrina did as he asked, Josh replaced the cardboard target with a wooden one.

He reloaded his gun with bullets from his belt as he approached. Snapping the cylinder closed, he took off his hat and stepped behind her, asking, "Which is your dominant hand?"

She lifted her right hand and he settled the handle of the gun against her palm, curling her fingers around it. "Just hold it like that for a sec," he said as he stepped flush with her backside and put his hands on her hips to turn them. "You're going to want to stand like this."

"Okay, now what?" she asked over her shoulder.

Instead of moving to her side like she expected him to do, he slid his arms under hers, lifting their arms together to show her the angle she should be holding each arm. "This hand will pull back the hammer and this one will hold the gun steady. Got it?"

Once she nodded, he said, "I'm going to put my hands over yours the first time, so you'll feel the kick and be prepared for it. Then you can do it yourself."

Sabrina faced the target and let her body melt into his arms. She enjoyed the feel of him surrounding her all over. She'd never felt so protected. "Ready."

"Now look down the barrel toward the target, then pull the hammer back." He demonstrated, then put the hammer back in place so she could do it.

Sabrina thumbed the hammer back, shifting the gun to center it on the target.

Josh slid his finger over hers near the trigger, while his other hand cupped hers under the handle. "You're going to want to aim down a tad, since these guns have a tendency to shoot up."

He tilted the gun down just a bit, then put pressure on her finger with his, pulling the trigger. When the gun went off, she flinched at the loud sound.

The bullet at least managed to hit the edge of the wooden target. She grimaced. "Er, sorry I jerked a little. The gun's much louder up close."

"Want to try it on your own?"

She nodded and cocked the hammer to advance another bullet in the chamber, then lifted her arms and positioned her hands around the gun like he'd shown her.

Josh hadn't moved from behind her, his warmth penetrating her clothes, seeping into her skin. She cut her gaze back to him. "Um, I am doing this on my own, right?"

He flashed a smile. "Of course."

Sabrina had expected him to move away, but she kind of liked the idea he was there to back her up if she needed it.

She started to lift her arms into a firing position when Josh's hands landed on her hips. He shifted them slightly, but instead of letting go once he was satisfied with her stance, he slid his hands up her waist, skimming the sides of her breasts before he ran his hands down her shoulders to adjust her arms.

"Better?" She sounded breathless. Clearing her throat, she blinked to regain focus and stop thinking about how much she enjoyed him touching her.

"Mmmm, much," he purred in her ear, resting his hands on her hips once more.

"Are you really trying to teach me?" she asked, raising an eyebrow.

"Just wanted to make your shooting lesson memorable," he said before he stepped to her side and folded his arms. "Take your shot, Annie O."

She smirked, then focused on the target and pulled the trigger. Before Josh could move, she thumbed back the hammer and took another shot, and then a few more until the bullets were gone.

Josh eyed the target and her shots' close grouping, then jerked a suspicious gaze her way. "I thought you said you've never shot a gun before?"

She shrugged. "I haven't shot a *real* gun, but I'm pretty good with the pellet variety. I was raised with two older brothers, remember?"

When Josh laughed, she said, "I heard you shooting earlier, but didn't get to see it. Why don't you show me your moves?"

His eyebrows shot up mischievously and he took a step closer. "My moves?"

She lifted the handle toward him, trying not to be drawn in by his suggestive undertone. "Reload, cowboy."

Josh's lips quirked as he took the gun. "I could easily run with that one too—"

She snickered. "Just show me what you've got."

His shoulders shook with amusement while he emptied the bullets. "You're killing me."

Sabrina smiled. Flirting with Josh felt so natural.

Once Josh loaded the gun, he started to lift it toward the target, but she gripped his arm and shook her head. Backing away to give him space, she said, "I want to see you draw and shoot. Why do I have this feeling you're darn good at it?"

His lips lifted in a cocky smile as he spun the gun into the gun belt holster without looking.

"Thought so," she murmured. "Go for it, cowbo—."

Before she finished speaking, he'd already drawn and unloaded all five bullets into the target.

Sabrina gaped. She couldn't believe how fast he'd moved. His hand was a blur, fanning back the hammer so fast between shots she hardly saw it. Shaking her head slowly, she exhaled a surprised breath. "Okay, I'm impressed."

"Then my job here is done," Josh said, flashing a grin before he spun the gun back into its holder once more.

Unbuckling the gun belt, he held it out to her. "Hold this for me while I help my family put away all this camp stuff."

Her fingers curled around the thick leather and gun handle so she wouldn't drop it. "I don't mind helping you clean up, Josh."

He quickly shook his head. "We've got it. Why don't you wait for me on the porch. I'll just be a few minutes."

Sabrina sat on the top step and spent ten minutes watching Josh and his family work together to put the stuff they'd built for the camp away in a storage shed beside the barn. While she watched, she absently ran her thumb over the gun's handle.

When she moved her finger along the bottom, the pad of her thumb seemed to catch on something. She glanced down and saw the initials NA had been etched into the metal.

Sliding the gun out, she inspected it closely and realized it was just like the gun in Josh's childhood bedroom. Probably part of a matching set. Who was NA?

What did Josh say the boy's name was in that picture in his room? He'd called him Nick Austin. She stared at the initials once more. If this is Nick's, then why does Josh take care of and use his friend's gun, but leaves his own gun untouched and collecting dust?

Sabrina lifted her gaze to watch Josh once more, only to find him standing on the bottom step staring at her running her thumb over the etching.

She could tell by his suddenly blank expression that he

didn't want to talk about it, so she slid the gun back into its holder and stood, holding the belt out to him.

Josh had put his hat back on, but she could see the look of hesitation in his eyes as if he was going to say something. Instead, he rolled his shoulders and walked the rest of the way up the stairs until he'd reached her level. Staring down at her, he took the gun belt and smiled. "Give me five minutes and we'll head out, okay?"

Once he went inside, Sabrina sat on the long porch swing and tried to picture what Josh's house would look like. She found it hard to conjure specific images, but one thing she knew for sure, it would be a cozy, comfortable place. Would he be a neat freak or a bit of a slob? She turned her face toward the warm sun and closed her eyes, looking forward to finding out.

"WAKE UP, SLEEPYHEAD."

Sabrina's eyes fluttered open and she quickly sat up, eyeing Josh, who'd apparently showered and changed into a white button down shirt and Wranglers, complete with a silver and gold buckle. "Was I asleep?"

Josh clasped her hand and pulled her to her feet. "Yep. You didn't get much sleep last night, so I'm not surprised you took a catnap."

He picked up her backpack and slung it over his shoulder. Ready to go?" His smile made the butterflies in her stomach multiply tenfold as he held his hand out to her. Wow, with the afternoon sun shining directly in his eyes, the teal color was downright arresting.

Josh squeezed her hand and pulled her toward the steps. When Sabrina saw a couple horses standing at the bottom of the stairs, she glanced his way. "We're not taking your truck?

He shook his head. "It's a nice day. Thought we'd take a ride to my place."

She squeezed his hand, her stomach knotting. "Um, I haven't gotten up the nerve to ride a horse yet. I was working my way up to that by grooming Lightning."

"Really?" Surprise flickered. "Okay, then." Releasing her hand, he called out to his nephew through the screen door, "Ben, can you put Queen away? Sabrina's going to ride with me."

Ben appeared at the door and nodded. "Sure thing Uncle Josh."

Sabrina shot him an apologetic smile, then followed Josh down the stairs to his horse.

"What's his name?" She rubbed the black horse's neck as Josh secured her small backpack behind the saddle.

Josh patted the animal's rump, then tugged on her hand to pull her toward him. "This here is Ace."

He'd barely released her hand before gripping her waist. Sabrina let out a yelp when he quickly lifted her across the horse's back. "Damn, you're so tiny I could put you in my pocket," he said softly as she settled into the saddle.

Sabrina felt so high up she gripped the saddle horn like a lifeline while Josh pulled himself up behind her.

Josh's arms came around her waist and he chuckled low in her ear. "Relax, Brina." Retrieving the horse's reins, he nudged Ace with his knees, and the horse turned around.

"Why aren't we taking the drive?" she asked, pointing toward the entrance to the Double K.

Ace headed for the back of the Kellys' house. Once the horse reached the edge of the property, Josh entered the woods, saying casually, "My place is this way. I've taken a couple of days off. As much as I'd like to say I'm doing this to watch over you, the truth is...I'd just like to spend some time alone with you."

"Oh," was all Sabrina got out before Ace began to climb the slight incline. The fact that Josh wanted her all to himself made her heart hammer, while the horse's movement upward forced her body to lean back against Josh. Being up so high still made her nervous. She tried to relax and let her head rest in the cradle of his shoulder, while her body settled against him as she slid back in the saddle.

Josh wrapped his arm around her waist and spoke in a low tone against her neck. "You're so tense. I can help you learn to enjoy riding if you'll let me."

She released an anxious breath. "Oh yeah, what's this technique called?"

"Distraction," he whispered seductively in her ear.

"Distraction, huh? Is this foolproof?"

"Only if you give yourself over to it." His arm around her waist tightened slightly. "Are you up for trying?"

Sabrina really wanted to overcome her fears. She blew out a tense breath and nodded.

As the horse walked at a plodding pace up the slope, Josh slid his hand to her belly. "What do you do when you're not visiting friends on vacation?"

She sucked in her breath when she felt his thumb slide along the underside of her bra in a slow, deliberate motion. How did the man sound so casual and laidback while he aroused her body with his tantalizing touch? She had to focus to answer. "I work in an advertising firm."

"Travel much with your job?" he asked at the same time he began to pull her tucked-in shirt from her jeans.

Her heart sped up. His purposeful, unhurried seduction made her want him that much more. It's like he was giving her time to change her mind. At any time, she could ask him to stop, but rational thoughts were fading fast, along with her fear of being high up on a horse. "Uh...um...no. Actually most of my job is done in the office. I only travel to a couple of meetings a year. Marketing isn't always as glamorous as it sounds."

"I was hoping you traveled to Texas a *lot*." He emphasized the last word as his fingers brushed against the bare skin just above the waistband of her jeans. Warmth began to spread through her body, competing with the Texas heat that clung to her even in the shade-covered trail.

"I haven't had a reason to travel this direction." Her voice trembled a little by the idea that he hoped to see more of her.

Josh suddenly clasped her waist tight. "I want to give you every reason tonight, Brina. Again and again."

His possessive hold, coupled with his sensual promise made it hard to focus on her surroundings. She glanced down to regain control, only to realize a moment's panic when Josh suddenly dropped the knotted end of the reins against Ace's neck and lowered his palms to her thighs.

"Josh, the reins," she gasped. Leaning over the saddle horn, she started to grasp the reins lying across Ace's neck when Josh quickly pulled her back against his chest.

"Ace knows the way," he replied, full of confidence. "I need both hands to learn every inch of this new territory I've never explored before on this trail," he whispered darkly before planting a tantalizing kiss on the sensitive spot behind her ear. The gentle brush of his lips on her skin caused a shiver to course through her, but the sensation of him slowly pulling the buttons apart on her shirt set her pulse racing.

As he flicked the last button and her shirt fell open, her stomach tightened in arousing anticipation while pressure rushed to the center of her body in pulsing tension.

When he cupped her breasts through her bra, Sabrina gripped the saddle horn tighter. She closed her eyes and waited with bated breath as her heartbeat thrummed in response.

The first brush of his thumbs across the swell of skin above the fabric of her bra made her gasp, but when he dipped his fingers past the cups' soft fabric to lightly run them over her nipples, pleasure shot straight down to her lower belly.

"Put your hands on my thighs," he suddenly said, the gruffness in his voice telling her he wasn't as calm as he let on.

Sabrina's eyes flew open. "No," she breathed out, jerking a panicked gaze to the ground as she clung to the saddle horn even more.

He twisted the front of her bra, popping it open. As his fingers gently traced her nipples, warm air kissed them, adding an unexpected layer of titillation that made them so sensitive she wanted to scream.

"Trust me, Sabrina," he seduced, then pinched the hard nubs.

The slight pain heightened her arousal, eliciting an unbidden moan before she could hold it back. He applied a bit more pressure and even though it only aroused her further, she got it. He wanted her to trust him. Slowly, she released her "lifeline," setting her hands on his thighs.

"That's my girl." Satisfaction laced his tone and he gently slid his thumbs back and forth over her nipples to ease the earlier sting. "Now lean your body fully against mine, close your eyes and feel."

She did as he requested, sinking into his warmth and closing her eyes.

When Josh's lips touched her neck, nuzzling her at the same time his hands cupped her breasts fully, she inhaled deeply, loving how he made her body respond to his every touch.

"Do you feel the horse moving under you, Brina? Feel his movements? Anticipate with your body and move with him, instead of against him." As he spoke, he traced a hand down her bare belly.

He was going to kill her with this slow sexual torture. She could only nod her answer. The tactile sensations of the horse swaying beneath her and his tender touch, combined with the scent of fresh outdoors, faint aftershave and leather melded into a provocative, arousing experience.

"I can feel how you're moving with Ace now." He sounded pleased, making her want to follow his next instruction. Slowly her body began to fully relax, moving with the horse's motion.

When she started to put her hands back on the saddle horn, he gripped her breast and belly tight, his body tensing behind her. "No, keep your hands on my thighs." His voice had lowered, turning darker as he moved his hand to her knee.

Her eyes opened once more. "What are you planning—" She sucked in an excited breath when he began to slowly massage her inner thigh.

"There's a lot I'm planning to do to you, darlin'," he drawled. Feathering his lips down her throat once more, he cupped the inside of her other thigh as well and applied pressure to both, pushing her legs further apart.

"Josh," she hissed out. Gripping his hard thighs, she tried to tighten her own thighs against the horse, but Josh's firm hold wouldn't let her. Instead he lifted her thighs and moved his muscular ones under hers, giving her the secure seat she sought.

"I would never let you fall, Brina. I'll always keep you safe."

He wanted her to fully put her trust in him. The only hold she had now was to depend on his thighs to keep her balanced. The throbbing anticipation was almost her undoing.

She let out a low moan while jolts of desire radiated from the center of her body. Her moan turned into a loud gasp when Josh's hold on her inner thigh tightened and this thumb slid along the seam of her jeans, straight across her throbbing center.

"When I touch you for the first time," he whispered in her ear. "I want to see your expression and the color of your eyes change." His grip on her breast tightened as he continued, "Do you want to know what I thought about last night while I lay on that damned couch?"

She could only nod while he leisurely brushed his thumb back and forth across her nipple, sending waves of desire curling from her breast straight down her body.

"I thought about pulling all your clothes off, taking my time so I could discover every inch of your sweet flesh," he said as the palm of his hand slid higher.

She bit her lip, anticipating, wanting him to touch her. The wait was agonizing.

Josh didn't skimp in the seduction department. She was

completely under his spell, her body a quivering, molten mass of nerves.

"I'd lay you down and run my hands all over your body. I'd touch you *everywhere*. Gentle you, nice and slow, then rev you up with each stroke across your soft skin. You'd arch your back, silently begging me to make my way to your breasts, then you'd lose control and tell me exactly what you wanted."

Gentle her? Holy shit. She felt anything but gentle. He made her feel wild and untamed. "You ah, really are the best riding instructor ever," she managed to get out.

A low, sexy laugh rumbled, then he continued in a seductive voice, "But I'd want to taste those rosy peaks instead." His breath warmed her ear as he slid both hands up her body to cup her breasts fully, his grip firm and possessive.

"I'd suck long and hard on each nipple, giving them equal time until you twisted and whimpered and pushed my head between your gorgeous thighs."

Sabrina's pulse thrummed. She missed the warmth of his hand so close to touching her. God, this man was the *best* at word foreplay. When his thumbs just barely brushed across her nipples, she squirmed, trying to assuage the painful ache that had settled between her legs, but he barely let her touch the saddle. Damn him!

"Then I'd move to your thighs and spread them wide, while my thumbs massaged your pink flesh. It'd turn me on to see just how wet you were for me. My mouth would start to water and I'd be unable to resist taking a long, leisurely taste with my tongue."

Sabrina dug her fingers deep into the side of his thighs underneath hers. *He's trying to kill me.*

"Easy, baby," he rasped, then slowly slid the flat of his warm palm down her stomach to cup her mound through her jeans.

Sabrina let out a whimper and his voice turned to velvet. "Like that, do you?" He applied slight pressure and continued in an aroused tone, "But one taste wouldn't be enough and I'd go back for more and more." His voice took on a relentless edge. "I'd trace every soft fold, every bit of your sensitive skin, making you so horny you'd beg me to make you come."

Sabrina's breathing turned choppy and her heart felt like it might beat right out of her chest. Wanton...that's how Josh made her feel.

Perched atop a horse, holding on to this sexy man's rock-hard thighs, his muscular chest and hard-as-marble erection pressed against her backside—all while his words and teasing touches built a fire burning inside her—she'd never been more turned on in her life.

"You're panting," he continued, his voice gruff. "I hope that's because you want this too. Tell me you want this," he demanded. His grip tightened on her sex at the same time he plucked at one of her nipples as if he wanted to make sure of her answer.

"Yes, I want this!" she breathed out in a hiss.

A rumble of male satisfaction sounded in his throat. "I can't wait to hear you scream when you come. I know you're a screamer, Brina, and fucking hell, all I thought of last night was hearing it."

Sabrina closed her eyes and moaned. His sudden intensity turned her on even more. The need for physical release engulfed her body, causing a sensual burn to rage and spiral inside her.

She didn't realize that she was rocking against his hand, until she felt the counter pressure of his palm and his pleased comment bleed through her consciousness, "That's it, baby. Damn, I can't wait to feel your sweet body wrapped around me."

When he suddenly folded his arms around her waist and set his chin on her shoulder, saying, "We're here," she realized his horse had stopped walking. Sabrina blinked her eyes open to try to regain some kind of control.

With her body still quaking, she managed a shaky smile as she took in the quaint house. His two-story wood-sided home with a bench swing off to the left of the front door and a couple of pale wood rocking chairs to the right created a homey look that surprised her considering he was a bachelor.

She noted that there wasn't a big front yard and about the same sized backyard with stables set on the far left corner. Woods stretched beyond the stables. Nodding to indicate the front yard that blended right into the woods, she said, "Now I know why you didn't drive me up here. Is there even a road to get to your place?"

Josh slid off the horse and retrieved his hat. Sliding his hat back on his head, he smiled. "Yeah, I guess the grass driveway you see appears to lead nowhere. We only used the road to bring up the materials to build my house, and then on the day I moved my stuff in. I prefer riding my horse, so the driveway has grown over by forest underbrush over time, but it's there." He pointed to the back yard. "There are open pastures beyond the woods behind my house. I just haven't cut a path to them yet."

Once he finished speaking, he reached up and clasped her around the waist. When he effortlessly lifted her off of Ace and set her on the ground, a gust of cool wind blew Sabrina's shirt open, pebbling her nipples. Heat suffused her face at the reminder she was standing there all brazen and bare breasted.

When she quickly re-snapped her bra, then pulled her shirt closed, Josh tilted her chin so he could see her face. "Are you blushing?"

She glanced away and fumbled with the buttons on her shirt in an effort to close it as quickly as possible. "I'm not usually so—"

"Free?" He clasped her arms and he pulled her against his chest so her hands were trapped between them. "I love that you can be your true self around me."

Her true self? This wasn't how she'd acted with other men she'd been with. Not at all. Her gaze snapped to his, but before she could decide how to respond, he released her and slowly buttoned the last few buttons for her.

"Sabrina," he began, resting his hands on her shoulders, where he rubbed his thumbs gently along her collarbone. "I want to get to know the real you. Don't hold back." His gaze held hers as he slid his hands down her back. Cupping her butt, he pulled her hips to his, a wicked smile crooking the corner of his mouth. "I certainly plan to share."

His quick-witted, sexy humor soothed her embarrassment, making her laugh.

Josh took off his hat and ran a hand through his hair, his penetrating gaze searching her face. A long, sexually charged moment passed between them, sweeping away her ability to speak.

Handing her the backpack he'd pulled off the horse, he said, "Why don't you go on inside and get comfortable while I put Ace away?"

Sabrina took her backpack and slipped it onto her shoulder. As she watched Josh walk Ace around the side of the house, she realized that she really did feel more comfortable riding Ace by the end of that ride. Smiling, she walked up the steps, then paused in the doorway before she walked inside.

The contemporary design showed her another side to Josh she wouldn't have expected. "Aren't you full of surprises, Josh Kelly," she murmured as she took in the kitchen and dining room, which sat on a two-step, raised up "island" in the center of the room. Josh must put an emphasis on cooking for his eating space to be such a large focal point in his home.

Shutting the door, her stomach pitched. God, she sure hoped he didn't expect her to cook. Eggs and toast were about all she'd learned to do. She'd always been in awe of her girlfriends who could just "whip up" a meal from practically nothing. Sabrina's creativity came in the form of advertising slogans and understanding target markets.

Even though Josh's choice for his kitchen placement seemed very modern and contemporary, he'd kept his place warm with rich leather and polished wood barstools against the tall wood and slate counters. Spindle back chairs graced the oval oak dining table. Wood floors spread across the entire house, giving it a welcoming feel.

To her left, the living room boasted a well-worn leather sofa and matching smaller two-seater sofa sitting on an Aztec design rug. Very few pictures graced the walls, but the ones that did depicted horses. Oils and watercolor pictures hung in the living room, while black and white photos of galloping horses decorated an office room off to her right.

Once again, Josh had added an Aztec rug in deep maroons and blues in the center of his office. A single mission style desk in a rich cherry wood and a tall black leather chair were the only pieces of furniture. A laptop, a printer/fax machine, and a telephone sat atop the desk.

Except for the few papers she'd seen on his desk, Sabrina just realized how utterly immaculate Josh's place was. She'd take a "neat freak" over a slob any day.

The backside of the main room held a foosball table in one corner and a poker table in the other. Her gaze followed the wrought iron spiral staircase against the center of the far back wall of the house. The staircase led to a small sitting area that overlooked the living space downstairs. It had a huge picture window, which probably had a gorgeous view of the woods behind the house.

On the far wall of the main floor, two doors led off on either side of the room, presumably to Josh's bedroom and a guest bedroom.

She bit her lip, wondering where she was supposed to freshen up. She felt sticky from the walk up the drive earlier. When her gaze landed on a door off to her immediate left, she saw a sink and smiled. Tugging her backpack strap higher, Sabrina walked into the bathroom to change clothes.

Josh's body ached for release while anticipation coursed through him. Sabrina's responsiveness set him on fire. The fact she let him take control revved him up, but he was the one who felt completely wrapped up in her. He couldn't wait to get back to his house, but he had to dial his desire back some. He'd scare the hell out of her if he yanked her into his arms and carried her straight to bed the moment he entered his house.

He forced himself to a slower pace as he walked Ace to the stables and opened the stall door.

After he pulled his horse inside and hung the saddle, he rifled through the saddle's pouch and retrieved his cell phone. Dialing Renee's direct line at the police department, he waited for her to answer.

"O'Hara speaking."

"Renee, this is Josh. Just wondering how the interrogation went with the guy who was caught last night. Did he confess to attacking Sabrina?"

"Nothing yet."

Her evasive tone irked him. He had to know the answer for sure. "So are you saying you still think it was him but he just hasn't confessed yet?"

"No."

"Wow, you're just full of information, aren't you?"

She sighed on the other end. "It's an investigation, Josh. I shouldn't even be talking to you about it. I'm hanging up now."

"Wait! C'mon, Renee," he cajoled. You can tell me."

"I'm not at liberty to say."

"Do you still skinny dip in the lake on the far side of the Masterson's estate? Oh, I think that you do."

"That's really low, Josh," she hissed, then lowered her voice. "How do you know about that?"

He smiled and leaned against the stall's doorway. "I'll tell you if you tell me."

Another big sigh came across the line. "Fine. We have to look at all scenarios, all motives. Considering the fire occurred while Colt and Elise were out of town...well, we have to investigate all possibilities."

"Such as?" he prompted, anxious for her to get to the point.

"We checked to make sure the homeowners' insurance hadn't been increased on the Lonestar property, up to and including a rider for additional fire hazard insurance."

"You're investigating insurance fraud?" he asked, incredulous. "I know it's been determined that the fire was set by the lantern, but that could've happened by accident when Sabrina was attacked."

"It could've been an accident," she agreed. "But as I said, we have to look at the possibility the person who attacked Sabrina wasn't the man we have in custody. The fact the stable door was locked points to premeditation. Based on our inquiries, Colt and Elise are clean on any recent changes to their homeowners' insurance, but we're still probing to rule any other scenarios out."

"You're barking up the wrong tree, Renee." Josh didn't bother to keep the harshness from his voice. "Keep me posted when the convict confesses."

"I wouldn't hold my breath. He's not talking. Okay, Josh, your turn. Who knows I skinny dip?"

She sounded so expectant, he couldn't keep the grin from his face. "Dirk."

"Dirk Chavez! Ohmigod, has he been watching me?" she asked, horrified.

"I don't know. You'll have to ask him." It was hard but Josh managed to suppress his amusement. Renee had always been known as a prude in school. The discovery she was less inhibited than she let on was entertaining. "Keep me in the loop on the investigation. I may be able to help."

"Will do."

Josh ended the call and left the stables, heading back to his house. As he mounted the porch stairs, his cell phone began to vibrate. Thinking it was Renee calling back, he was surprised to see Colt's name on the caller ID.

"Hey, Colt. How's Elise's dad doing?"

"He's a tough bull. Doing better now. Elise and I wanted to see how Sabrina was doing."

"She appears to be fine." Josh tried to sound casual when all he could think about was spending time alone with Sabrina. Better to get this out of the way now. "Actually, she's staying with me for a couple of days. So if Elise needs to reach her, tell her to call my cell."

"Elise will be glad to know Sabrina's being watched over. Tell her we'll be home as soon as we can. Oh, and Josh, do me a favor and keep an eye on the ranch, will ya? I don't like being gone with no one there watching the place. You know Jackson's ways."

"Sure thing, Colt."

He was just about to hang up when Colt said, "One last thing. We appreciate you looking out for Sabrina, but you'd better not hurt her or you'll have me to contend with."

Josh set his jaw, then answered, "I told you I'd keep her safe, Colt. The rest is none of your damned business."

6

Sabrina slipped into her black and white floral patterned miniskirt and a white fitted v-neck sleeveless summer sweater. Its vee plunged low, revealing her cleavage, small as it was. She inhaled and turned sideways, puffing her chest out, then shrugged at her less-than-voluptuous silhouette. If the man wanted large boobs, he'd have to look elsewhere. Nothing on her body fell in the "supersize" category.

Checking her image in the mirror once more, she slid the rubber band out of her long braid and shook out her hair. As she ran her brush through the thick black mass, now wavy from the braid, she smiled at the sensation of her hair flowing behind her. Because her hair was halfway down her back, she usually pulled it up to keep it out of the way. Running her fingers all the way to the tip ends of her hair caused her thoughts to shift to one of the last conversations she had with her old boyfriend.

"Why don't you just cut it all off?" Jeremy had asked one morning while she pulled her hair up.

She let the clip lock onto the hair piled on her head. "I just can't bring myself to part with it, I suppose."

"Seems like a nuisance to me," Jeremy said, shrugging like he couldn't care less.

Shaking her irritation away as she came back to the present, she met her green gaze in the bathroom mirror. "Ready to go headlong, Bri? No reservations, no hang-ups. Just you and Mr. Sex-on-Wheels...doing well, almost-sex-on-a-horse and wherever else we can think of." Which wasn't such a bad idea, she thought with a grin as she turned and walked out of the bathroom.

The pep in her steps slowed as she made her way back into the main living area of Josh's home. With its rich earth tones, deep blues and shades of maroon, it really was a very homey house—the kind of house she could see herself living in. *Don't even go there, sister*. It's just that thinking about having guilt-free sex with Josh would make more sense in a hotel room, not his warm, cozy home.

She almost turned around in her high-heeled sandals and hightailed it back to the bathroom to change clothes into something less revealing until she spotted Josh leaning against the fireplace. His elbow rested on the wood mantel and he was staring out the large picture window.

The sound of her heels gave her presence away. Josh turned and his teal green gaze burned a slow, lingering path down her chest to her legs and then back up. "You changed."

"The heat of the day made me feel all rumpled, so yeah, I changed."

His appreciative smile faded slightly and he spread his hands. "Since you're all dressed up, would you like to go out somewhere? We could go to Rockin' Joes and dance if you'd like."

Not tonight! She glanced around his home. "Right here is great. You have a gorgeous place."

"I have an idea." Josh pulled off his hat, then tossed it on the coffee table. He picked up a remote from the table and hit a couple of buttons.

Music began to flow throughout the house. A slow song full of soul.

He set the remote down and started toward her, his pace sure, unhurried. He looked entirely too sexy for his own good with rolled up shirtsleeves revealing corded, muscular forearms and hard working hands that she knew from experience could be so very gentle. With each step he took, his belt's large gold and silver buckle accentuated his slim hips and long legs. The man literally made her mouth water. Sabrina swallowed and her heart pounded. God, was she in trouble.

Josh's expression shifted from determined to intense as he closed the distance between them and captured her hand. Pulling her to the center of the living room, he wrapped an arm around her waist and stepped right up to her. As the music thrummed its seductive rhythm, Josh began to move, turning her around.

"We're dancing?" she asked, relaxing a little.

He nodded, his hand splaying along her lower back. "One of my many talents."

She held his gaze. "Let's see, sharpshooter, horse whisperer, damsel rescuer, and now," she paused as he twirled her around then pulled her back into his arms, "excellent dancer."

"Told you so," he said, adopting a smug smile.

"And modest too."

Josh smirked, eyes darkening as he tugged her even closer. "Never claimed that one, darlin'. Not once."

They danced to a couple more songs and even though the music ended, Josh kept dancing as if it hadn't. Sabrina smiled and tapped his chest. "Um, the music stopped."

Josh finally stopped moving and released her, but he didn't move away. His gaze lowered to her mouth, then he shifted it back to her eyes. "I could make steaks. Are you hungry?"

Sabrina shook her head. "I'm not really hungry right now."

When Josh's gaze strayed to her mouth once more, she bit her lip and took a step back. "Are you hungry?"

"Ravenous." His eyes flashed to hers, flaring with heat as he stepped toward her.

Sabrina took a few steps back, enjoying the out-of-control feeling of being stalked by Josh. When the backs of her shoes hit the wall's wooden baseboard, she tried her best to control her rapid breathing.

Josh put a hand on the wall above her head and pressed up against her body, sliding his jean-clad thigh between hers as if he had every right to put it there.

Sabrina stared at his chest until his finger lifted her chin so she had to meet his gaze.

As his thumb traced her lips, her chest rose and fell to her rapid heartbeat. But when his fingers slowly feathered down her chin and then her throat, continuing to descend lower, she held back the urge to pant, but damn that's exactly what he made her do. She wanted this...him...that much.

The sensation of his work-roughened finger tracing the vee of her sweater, touching her bare skin while his gaze held hers, made it hard not to shake.

"Touch me, Brina," he said, his tone gruff and full of desire, the teal shade in his eyes turning the color of a churning, stormy ocean.

Sabrina pulled the snaps open on his shirt, then slid her hands under the open flaps and laid her palms against his warm skin. When the muscles underneath her hands flexed, the power behind his hard-working body was more than intoxicating. It was addictive, she thought as she explored his corded chest, then slid her fingers down his abs.

At the same time she ran her hands around his waist, Josh's finger brushed the swell of her breast, then slowly dipped in between the cleavage her bra created.

Sabrina sucked in her breath as he added another finger and the corner of his lip quirked upward. His movements were slow and seductive right up until he bent his fingers, hooked them around her bra and yanked her forward.

She let out a surprised gasp and her hands fell to his belt loops. All she could do was hold on as he cupped the back of her neck and arched her toward his descending mouth.

Josh's lips brushed slowly along hers once in a teasing, sexual dance before his mouth claimed hers in a hot, passionate, possessive kiss. While his tongue slid against hers, his hand spread over her breast, cupping it. When she sighed at his touch, he took advantage of the break in their kiss, biting at her lower lip as his thumb rubbed across the hardened bud through her bra, teasing her, taunting her, making her want him more.

Desire swirled from her breast down to her lower belly. Sabrina gripped his hips, pulling him closer, moaning against his mouth. Josh growled low in his throat and dropped his hands to her rear, cupping her in a tight hold. He slid his thigh higher until he hit her center, then pulled her against him, breasts to chest, hips to hips.

She cried out when he pushed her against the wall and replaced his thigh with his body. He rubbed his erection against her entrance through their clothes, rocking his hips in a slow, erotic thrust as his lips lowered to her throat.

"Damn, you jack me up, Brina. I've never wanted a woman as much as I want you," he rasped against her throat. His fingers flexed on her rear right before he lifted her body off the ground so he could fit himself fully against her. She moaned as he ground against her, buckle, jeans and all.

"The feeling's entirely mutual," she breathed out, gripping his muscular shoulders. The buckle pressed against her lower belly, its cool pressure stimulating her heated skin. Rough jeans rubbed against her sensitive thighs and thin underwear, while knowing hands slid up the back of her bare legs. The tactile sensations and her amped up anticipation combined with the smell of leather, creating the ultimate sensory aphrodisiac. Her sex throbbed and her breasts ached as she clutched his shoulders. Wrapping her legs around his trim waist, she met each jerk of his hips with counterpressure ones of her own.

"Oh God, Josh, I'm going to lose it if you don't stop now," she hissed out as her body tightened with her impending climax.

"I sure as hell hope so, baby. It'll be the first of many," he said, his voice darkly promising. She felt his hot breath on her neck and heard his own breathing increase.

When he bit lightly on her throat, Sabrina shattered. She clung to his shoulders as her orgasm slammed through her, shocked by the realization that having sex with her clothes on could be so heart-stoppingly erotic and seductively sensual. Josh didn't stop moving against her until her gasps of delight quieted and the only sound in the room was their heavy breathing.

Sabrina laid her head back against the wall while Josh dropped his forehead to her heaving chest. She ran her hands through his thick, wavy hair, holding him close. Her movements released the masculine scent of his shampoo. She smiled, loving that his hair felt as soft as she thought it would.

He'd surprised her when he didn't immediately try to get her naked and in his bed. Instead, he'd given her what she desired without taking what he obviously needed. The unselfish gesture melted her heart. Without thinking, she bent and kissed him on the top of his head.

Josh pressed his lips against the swell of one of her breasts, then lifted his head, his gaze focused and full of new purpose. Straightening, his hands clasped her buttocks to hold her against him as he walked over to the sofa. He kissed her on the jaw before putting his knee on the couch to lower her onto the cushions.

Standing up, he held her gaze as he pulled off his shirt. Sabrina's breathing kicked up at her first sight of his fully naked chest in the light of day. Wide-shouldered and lean-hipped, the man stole more than her control. He took her breath away. When he started to lower his body over hers, she put her foot up, pressing her sandal's heel against his chest. She lifted her eyebrow. "Aren't you forgetting something?"

Josh looked down at her shoe and with a sinful smile ran his fingers up her leg until he reached the buckle of her sandal. Once he'd removed it, he lifted her other ankle. While he unbuckled the strap on her other shoe, Sabrina set her bare foot on his chest.

There was something so sensual about the pad of her foot resting on his warm skin. She wiggled her toes against the hard surface and smiled when he winked at her.

Shoes removed, Josh encircled her ankles with his fingers. His hands felt so big against the small bones, his action reminded her just how much larger he was than her. Josh's teasing expression turned serious as he slid his hands along her calves. When he reached her thighs, a hungry look settled on his face. He massaged the sensitive insides of her legs and slowly pushed them apart.

The sight of his nostrils flaring as he stared down at her panties made Sabrina's belly clench in excitement. She held her breath and her heart began to hammer as his fingers brushed against her damp underwear. "So responsive," he murmured, the expression on his face full of desire and thoroughly focused as he touched her through her underwear. Her pulse began to thunder in her ears when his thumb began to rub the highly sensitized flesh in small circles.

He acted like he was in complete control while she felt like she would fly apart at any moment. Sabrina wanted him to feel as out of control as she felt, so she arched up and grabbed his belt buckle with one hand and his package with the other and lifted herself slightly off the couch, teasing, "You're just as responsive."

Her aggressive action had surprised him and Josh's breath came out in a ragged hiss. Closing his eyes for a brief second, he placed his hand over hers, then slid her hand along his rock-hard erection.

When she curled her fingers tighter, applying pressure, his

eyes snapped open, full of raging desire. "No, not yet." Pulling her hand away, he reached under her skirt, saying in a gruff tone, "Lift your hips, baby. I have to taste you."

"Josh," she began while she complied with his request. Touching his hair as he slid her underwear down her legs, she continued, "You've got to be ready to explode. Enough. You've proven how easily you can make me fly apart."

Taking his hand, she pressed his fingers against her naked flesh and finished in a breathless whisper, "I'm ready for you, cowboy."

Josh froze, his shoulders tense, gaze focused on his hand pressed against her heat.

Ever so slowly, he eased a finger inside her.

His intimate touch shook her deeply, and it took everything she had not to move, not to react. Sabrina bit her lip to hold her moan back, but when he started to pull his finger out, the thought of him severing their connection even for a second ripped an unexpected mewl of disappointment from her.

His head snapped up and his jaw set as their gazes locked. Josh withdrew his hand from her body and quickly unbuckled his belt, pulling it through the loops.

As the belt's buckle clattered against the hardwood, he yanked the top button of his jeans open. His I've-got-to-have-her-right-fucking-now reaction sent a flush of renewed heat rushing along her skin. When Josh leaned over her, the muscles in his arms bunched and she couldn't resist touching them before she reached between their bodies to finish unbuttoning his fly.

The phone rang, causing her to pause.

Josh breathed through his nose and shook his head in fast jerks as if he were trying to regain focus. His expression took on a tortured, ravenous look as he glanced at her lips. He leaned closer, his mouth a breath away from hers. "You'll never know the benefits of taking it slow if you don't let me show you, darlin'."

He moved away from her mouth and planted a kiss on the curve of her breast. The phone continued its incessant noise, each ring punctuating his seductive descent down her body as he lifted her sweater and kissed her belly, then moved to brush his lips against her navel before he slid lower and pressed her skirt higher so he could nuzzle the bit of dark hair between her legs.

Before he lowered his head to taste her, his gaze met hers once more. "I want to enjoy you before I lose total control, Brina. God knows once I'm inside this warm, sweet body of yours, it'll take all the concentration I have to take it slow with you."

His answering machine picked up, but Sabrina was too caught up in his toe-curling declaration to pay much attention to it. She nodded and relaxed her thighs, giving him full access to her body.

Josh didn't say another word as he slid his hands under her skirt and clasped her bare bottom in a firm hold. Lifting her hips slightly, he lowered his mouth to her damp flesh.

Josh's tongue had just made a long swipe from her center all the way to her clitoris, when a voice came across his answering machine.

"Kelly, answer the damn phone so I can chew your good-for-nothing ass out. Why the hell did you tell Renee I've seen her skinny-dipping? I just got this phone call from her..."

"*Dirk Chavez, keep your peeping-tom eyes to yourself. I can arrest your sorry ass, you know.*"

Switching back to his own voice, Dirk continued, "Thanks for rattin' me out. Just because you put in inhumanly crazy extra hours at the station doesn't mean I can't convince the chief to give you hose-cleaning duty the next time you're at the firehouse."

Once he'd finished his rant, Dirk let out a vengeful laugh. "Better get that bristle brush ready. Call me, ya freakin' turncoat." Then he hung up.

Sabrina's eyebrows shot up and her heart jerked at the surprising information. She recognized Dirk's name. And the fact he was a firefighter, coupled with his comments on the answering machine, made her think Josh was too. Damn it to hell!

Josh must've misunderstood her raised eyebrows. "Had to out him. It was for a good cause." He grinned before he lowered his head toward her body once more.

But Sabrina put her hand on his head. Stopping his descent, she tried to scoot back on the couch.

Questions flashed in Josh's eyes as he tightened his grip on her butt.

"You're a firefighter?" she managed to squeak out, while a cold sweat washed over her body.

He nodded, his expression shifting to concern. "What's wrong, Sabrina?"

She couldn't do it—couldn't let him start something that she wouldn't allow herself to finish. The magnetic pull he held over her was just too freaking strong. She liked him too much already.

"Maybe this wasn't such a good idea," she said in a flat tone.

Why the hell didn't Elise tell her? The frantic thought

flitted through her mind as Josh continued to stare at her like he couldn't believe what she was saying. *I'm going to kick her ass*, she mentally swore with conviction. When the blush of shock finished rolling through her, self-preservation kicked in and she shoved at Josh's chest.

Taken by surprise, Josh let go of her and slid off the couch onto his knees.

Sabrina quickly stood and turned to walk away.

Before she knew what happened, she was flat on her stomach, lying half on the hardwood floor and half on the area rug. Josh held her arms stretched over her head with one strong hand while his hard body lay across her back, his thigh pressed between hers.

He shifted slightly and his hand slid under her skirt, cupping her ass as he bit out next to her ear, "I damn well know you want me, Brina. So when the hell did my being a firefighter fall below the rank of just a plain old cowboy?"

She heard the anger in his voice and couldn't believe how turned on she was by his aggressiveness.

His fingers grasped her butt as he continued, his whiskers tickling her cheek. "If you've had a change of heart about us," he said as he slid his fingers closer to her entrance, not touching her but hovering very close. "Then I can accept that, but if you're pushing me away because of what I do..." He paused to brush his fingers across her labia. It was the barest of touches, but oh-so intentional, then continued, his voice, low, angry and full of tension, "Now *that* I won't accept."

She closed her eyes, shocked by his fine-tuned playing of her body, at how, with the slightest touch, he made her want him to touch her, to slide his fingers inside her. Even as she struggled to free her wrists, she couldn't help involuntarily arching, spreading her legs, or the thrill that zipped through her body at being held while he touched her as intimately as he wanted.

He slid his finger down her slit, then paused. Circling her entrance in a slow methodical movement, he kissed her neck and said in a controlled tone, "I'm waiting for your answer."

All the things she'd told herself about this trip floated through her head: *No inhibitions, don't hold back no matter if he wouldn't normally be a man you'd date. If he trips your trigger, go for it*! "You're killing me," she gasped between pants.

He didn't move, just held his tense body against her and grated, "I need your answer."

She nodded.

"Hell no! I want to hear it, Brina," he snapped, his grip on her wrists tightening.

Josh took control but also gave it back to her. It's like he just "got" her. "Yes, I want you."

She'd barely gotten the words out when he aggressively slid two fingers deep inside her.

As a wave of hot desire shot through her, he spoke against her ear. "You know why that feels so good? Because we're right." He withdrew, this time slowly pressing back inside her, his movements tantalizingly erotic as he pressed a kiss to her neck and murmured, "So fucking right."

The emotion in his comment, coupled with his tender touch, sent goose bumps scattering along her skin. No one she'd ever been with had ever made her feel so many emotions at once. No one had even come close.

Josh moved his body off hers and let go of her wrists. Lying down beside her, he clasped her thigh in a firm hold and said in a husky tone, "I want to finish what we started. Will you let me, Brina?"

Sabrina inwardly sobbed at the intense throbbing that had commenced once he'd pulled his fingers away. Josh loosened his hold on her to let her roll onto her side to face him on the carpet.

Holding his deep teal gaze, she lifted to pull her sweater off and toss it on the floor. His gaze followed hers when she clasped his hand and cupped his palm against her, saying, "Finish what you started."

The tension in Josh disappeared, but when his gaze locked on her white lace bra, his eyes darkened and a different kind of tension flowed through him. He reached for the waistband of her skirt and as he slid the smooth material down and off her body, he spoke in a barely controlled tone, "Take off your bra, baby. I want to see every inch of your bare flesh."

Sabrina's heart raced and she bit her lip in anticipation as she shrugged out of the lacy material and tossed it on her discarded sweater.

The late afternoon sun shone through the large picture window across the room, bathing Josh's blond hair and sculpted torso in a golden glow. She wanted to run her hands all over the hard planes and cut angles defining his chest and broad shoulders.

Josh leaned up on his arm and put the flat of his other hand between her breasts. Slowly he slid his palm down the middle of her body until he reached her lower belly. The primal look on his face as his gaze trailed down her skin, as if he wanted to devour her, turned her insides to mush.

Sliding his hand sideways at her waist, he spread his

fingers wide, surprise creasing his brow. "You're so tiny I can literally span your body with my hand."

"Don't let the small package fool you, Kelly," she replied in a playful yet stern voice. "I'm made of sturdy stock."

She'd barely gotten the comment out before Josh was lying across her body, his hands holding hers above her head once more.

A wicked smile curled his lips, his eyes darkening. "I'm counting on it, darlin'."

7

Josh's mouth crashed against hers, his kiss deep and thorough as his tongue sparred with hers. Sabrina tried to tug her hands free, to hold him close, but he held firm, lacing his fingers with hers in a tight grip. His lips trailed a burning path to her jaw and then her throat, while his hands slid down her arms even as he continued to hold them above her head.

Sabrina arched her back when he flicked his tongue across her hard nipple, then moaned deep in her throat as he sucked hard on the sensitive nub. The tug of his mouth caused an aching throb to shoot straight to her sex and a new round of goose bumps to form on her skin.

She sighed in pleasure and tried once again to free her arms to touch him.

"Not yet, Brina," he said against the curve of her skin before he moved to her other breast and lavished the nub with the same attention.

"Bend your knees," he ordered gently as he released her arms so he could trail his lips down her abdomen.

As she bent her knees, Sabrina threaded her fingers through his blond wavy hair, gently tugging the softness against her palms. Josh surprised her when his big hands slid down her chest and cupped her breasts.

He gave her a devilish grin as he twirled her nipples between his fingers. She could only gasp and close her eyes while desire swirled in her belly.

His hair slipped from her fingers a second before he laved at her entrance with his tongue. She bucked and gasped.

Josh said in a calm tone, "Easy, baby, I just want to love on you."

Sabrina tried not to think about the women he must've used the same technique on as he nuzzled her mound, then found her clit with his tongue. *Stop thinking. Just soak up the experience.*

Letting the tension ease out of her, she gave in to feeling as Josh took long, leisurely swipes against her sex. When his tongue slid inside her and he pinched her nipples at the same time, she keened her excitement, thrilled by the dual combination.

Panting, she slid her fingers in his hair once more and arched her back. Then Josh kissed his way to her clit and mumbled, "You're so sweet. I love the way you taste." Right before he sucked hard on the swollen bit of flesh.

Her entire body shook with pent-up sexual tension, needing release. When Josh let go of one of her breasts then slid two fingers deep inside her and began stroking her hot spot, Sabrina moaned and dug her toes in the carpet underneath her.

"Oh, God, Josh, yes...but," she panted, then gave a nervous laugh.

"What?" He lifted his head and met her gaze as he continued to stroke her body. "Do you feel like you want to pee?"

She nodded and bit her lip.

His smile turned carnal, the kind of smile that would melt women where they stood. "Then I'm hitting the right spot. You're going to come. Long and hard. Let go, baby, and feel," he rasped before he lowered his head to her body and laved at her clit once more.

Sabrina ached so desperately, her body shuddered with the feelings rocking through her. Damn he was making her feel things she'd never experienced before. She was glad she didn't hold back with Josh. It felt so good to let him take complete control. This is what she wanted. Exactly what she needed.

Josh let go of her breast and moved a hand to cup her buttock, pulling her closer. He briefly lifted his head and said in a rough voice, "Give in, Brina. Come for me, darlin'. This sexy body of yours was made for lovin'. Show me just how much."

When he finished, he kissed her inner thigh, then pressed his thumb on her clitoris while his thrusts continued to heighten her bliss, harder, deeper, more aggressive with each stroke.

Sabrina rocked against him, her heart racing. When her orgasm slammed through her, each wave more intense than the last, she pressed closer to him, her rapid breathing and sighs of release cutting through the silence in the room.

After she quit moving, Josh moved quickly above her, his mouth covering hers in a scorching kiss. She tasted her own salty sweetness and welcomed the aggressive thrust of his tongue against hers, telling her just how ready he was to be inside her.

She reached between them and pulled at the buttons on his jeans until they were all undone. Pushing at his waistband, she pressed her lips against his neck, telling him without words how much she wanted him.

Josh stood and shrugged out of his jeans and underwear. Before he tossed his jeans aside, he pulled a condom out of the pocket. Sabrina sighed inwardly, appreciating his perfectly muscled thighs and calves, but when her gaze landed on his impressive erection as he rolled on the condom, her belly tensed in anticipation.

Once Josh knelt between her legs and she got a closer view of him, she realized he was much thicker than any man she'd been with and she was pretty sure he was longer too. She bit her lip as apprehension gripped her. When his knee nudged her thighs further apart, she caught the expression on his face—the intensity and sheer concentration. He was on the edge of losing control.

Grasping Josh's shoulders, Sabrina swallowed her nervousness and tried to relax as he eased his erection against her. She felt the tension in his shoulders, saw his focused expression, and heard his breathing turn shallow as he pushed further inside her.

She ached everywhere but especially where they connected. She tensed when his fullness began to stretch her, turning the ache to a burning sensation.

"Relax..." he grated out, then paused, closed his eyes and blew out a breath. After a couple of moments, his sexy teal gaze locked with hers once more and he finished in a ragged tone, "You're so tight. You've got to relax for me, baby, or I'm going to hurt you."

Sabrina took a deep breath and released a nervous giggle. "This is one time when being small in stature might be a *real* pain in the ass."

Josh flashed a grin, but amusement quickly fled his expression as the sexual tension amped between them. He withdrew and grasped her hips. Tilting her body, he pressed back in once, twice, three times, rocking into her.

"You can take me, Brina. I know you can," he encouraged while priming her body in slow, rhythmic movements.

She closed her eyes and arched her back, soaking in the amazing sensations rippling through her. Heat flowed between them with each tantalizing thrust, easing his entrance. Once his penetration moved deeper, Josh laid his sweat-soaked chest on hers and grated, "Holy hell you feel good," then thrust hard, seating himself fully inside her.

Sabrina gulped back a yelp of discomfort as the full breadth of him invaded her.

Josh jerked his head up and cupped her face, concern in his eyes. "Are you okay?"

She nodded and gripped his shoulders, wrapping her legs around his trim waist. "Now show me what you got and don't hold back. With all this anticipation you've built up, I have high expectations."

"I'll do my best not to disappoint," Josh said in a rush of breath, then withdrew and slammed into her, giving her exactly what she asked for.

"Yes!" she cried out and dug her nails into his shoulders. He hitched higher, adding pressure and the rough rub of his body stimulated hers, setting off a series of small tremors deep inside.

Josh dipped his head and nuzzled her neck, saying close to her ear, "Told you we're right; a perfect fit. I feel every little tremble, every muscle clench against my cock, and it's making me crazy. I can't wait to hear that scream when you come."

He rocked his hips and she moved with him, breathing out, "I'm not one to scream, Josh."

His laugh came out in a harsh bark. "Guess I'm one lucky bastard then. I can't believe the men you've been with didn't know the wildcat they had on their hands." Grasping her hips, he tilted her just so and new arousing sensations shot through her. "I fucking love that I get to bring it out of you!"

With his last words, his grip on her hips tightened and his strokes turned more dominant and aggressive. After a particularly forceful downward thrust, he ground his body against hers and demanded, "Let me hear it, Brina!" And that was all it took.

Sabrina dug her nails into his back and whimpered when her orgasm started, then she couldn't hold back her scream any longer. She wrapped her arms tight around his neck and pulled him close as she lifted her hips against his body, hoping to drag out the soul-deep, body-rocking sensations as long as possible.

Josh cupped the back of her neck and gave a low groan as he came on the tail end of her orgasm. Once he stopped moving against her and his heart rate slowed, he shrugged his shoulders and grunted, his smile smug. "Well, hello, kitty-cat."

When he dipped his shoulder and she saw the deep red claw marks she'd inflicted, heat rushed to her cheeks. "I'm so sorry, Josh."

He clasped her chin when she tried to look away, his expression intense. "You didn't hold back. That's what I want!" His hold loosened and his gaze softened. "Sabrina, that was...no words can describe—"

"So let's not try," she said quietly as an ache settled in her chest. She didn't want it to mean more. She already knew she'd be pining after Josh the minute she left Texas. She didn't need the memory of his heartfelt words reminding her just how spectacular they were together haunting her every thought.

Josh gave her a puzzled look, then supported his weight on his forearms on either side of her. "Why was my being a firefighter a problem?"

She shrugged and tried for a light tone. "It's not a problem."

"Not buying it," he countered, his blond brows slashing downward.

"Really, it's fine, Josh."

When she tried to slide out from under him, he didn't budge. "I'm not letting you up until you tell me."

He suddenly felt much heavier. He'd meant what he said. He wasn't moving. Sabrina sighed. "My father was a firefighter. He died fighting a fire. It happened while I was...away at college." She tried to say the last as unemotionally as possible, but instead, she choked on the last few words.

By the time she finished speaking, all the color had drained from Josh's face. He gently cupped her jaw, his own tense. "God, I'm such an ass. I'm sorry, Sabrina."

Her chest constricted. She appreciated his concern. "It's okay. You didn't know."

Josh rolled over and pulled her into his arms. Kissing the top of her head, he said, "Do you want to talk about it?"

She shook her head, then rubbed her nose against his warm chest, soaking in his masculine smell. "There's nothing to tell."

He squeezed her slightly until she met his gaze. He searched her face with a doubtful look, then nodded. "You'll tell me when you're ready."

Sabrina lowered her head back to his chest and absorbed the sensation of his hard muscles under her cheek as he ran his fingers through her hair. "That feels good," she murmured.

He lifted some strands, turning them toward the light. "I love your hair, how the sun reflects off the blue highlights in it. I like it best flowing down your back."

She tried to turn and winced. Some of her hair had caught under her shoulder. Shifting, she pushed it out from under her, a wry smile on her lips. "Sometimes it can get in the way. My old boyfriend wanted me to cut it."

His gaze locked with hers. "I'd love to shake his hand."

Her eyes widened and she met his gaze. "Why?"

"To tell him thank you for being such an idiot. I might never have met you otherwise."

"Thank you for the compliment." She smiled and closed her eyes, loving his tender touch as he ran his fingers from the top of her head all the way to the ends of her hair.

"As for your hair," he began, then fisted his hand in the mass and gently tugged until her eyes fluttered open. "Don't cut it off. I love it long."

The seductive look in his gaze made her breasts ache and her body throb all over again. "I won't," she said breathlessly.

"The length has some definite advantages," His voice turned gruff as he used his hold on her hair to pull her close and steal a kiss.

Sabrina let out a quiet, swooning sigh against his mouth, amazed by how easily Josh exuded the kind of raw sexiness that made her feel like the most desired woman in the world.

When his mouth started to slant harder against hers and her stomach rumbled, Sabrina giggled in embarrassment.

"Are you ready for that steak now?" he teased.

"Oh, crap, I just remembered," she said, glancing at her watch.

Josh frowned. "What?"

She pressed a light kiss to his mouth. "As much as I would love to spend the rest of the day in bed with you, I promised Nan we'd come for an early dinner."

"Tonight?"

He looked so displeased she couldn't help but laugh. "Yes, tonight."

"Doesn't she know we're on a date?"

Her lips quirked and she glanced down at their naked bodies. "Is that what this is?"

"You know what I mean." His brow furrowed and he ran a finger down her chest and along the curve of her breast. "I want you all to myself."

His touch sent butterflies scattering through her belly. "I'm pretty sure you're going to be subjected to intense scrutiny of your intentions toward me, Nan-style, so be prepared to dodge and segue like a champ. I think with Elise gone, she's adopting the 'look out for Sabrina's well-being' role."

When he sighed heavily, she shrugged. "Don't sweat it. I'm not, but I did promise her, so we're going."

"What do you mean, 'you're not'?"

She swept her hair over her shoulder and set her chin on

his chest. "Just that I'm a big girl. I don't need anyone to worry about my feelings."

When she moved to get up, Josh clasped her arm and yanked her back down and across his chest until they were nose to nose. "What if *I* want to know about your feelings?"

Was he being sincere or teasing her? She mentally shook herself, thinking she must've read more into his comment than he meant. Pulling back a little, she rolled her eyes and patted his chest. "Don't worry, Josh. I absolve you of the burdensome responsibility of safeguarding my heart." She gave a sly smile and traced her finger along the light hair that ran down his abdomen. "But I'll happily give you the key to my chastity belt later. "So, come on, lazybones. The sooner we go, the sooner we can get back."

While Ace followed the path through the woods that led to the Lonestar, Josh was thankful for the shade the trees provided. That way he didn't have to put a hat on Sabrina's head to protect her from the heat. Selfishly, he wanted her as close as he could get her and a hat's brim would just get in the way.

Pulling Sabrina against him, he breathed in the floral scent of her shampoo and her natural sweet smell and was surprised at the way the scent made him feel. He felt content, happy, and horny—in that order. Sabrina seemed more at ease riding this time, and he was sure the fact she had changed back into a comfortable pair of jeans for their ride helped.

As Ace walked down the wooded path, the underbrush

crunching under his hooves, Sabrina laid back against his chest, sighing in contentment. With the flashes of sunlight streaking through the trees, adding to the beautiful silence in the forest, Josh couldn't resist kissing her temple as a feeling of rightness settled over him. Sabrina was everything he wanted in a woman—sexy, uninhibited, responsive, strong of heart and challenging.

When she told him about her dad, he felt a familiar stab in his chest. The memory of Nick came rushing back as if it were yesterday, making his heart twist and his gut knot in regret. They'd had so much fun that late fall day, trying out their new Halloween costumes. He and Nick had played into the early evening, until their parents had called them home. Promising to meet at their fort the next day, like they did every day, they'd gone home. Nick never made it to the fort the next day.

Josh shrugged off the melancholy memory. Instead he focused on the sexy woman in front of him and just how much she'd come to mean to him in such a short time. When he was with Sabrina, he didn't feel the driving need to be at the fire station at all hours. No woman in his past had ever done that to him. With her in his arms, his sense of duty, which he'd never been able to turn off before, shifted to the back of his mind for a while.

What he felt for Sabrina went far beyond anyone he'd ever been with. He couldn't believe how protective and possessive he felt about her. Damn. He knew he was jumping the gun. For all he knew she didn't feel the same about him. No doubt they were sexually compatible, but he wanted more than just a few days with her. He wanted to give them a chance. Would she? One thing he knew for certain...he had a hell of a hurdle to jump with her past.

How could he overcome her reservations about dating a fireman? The loss of her father in a fire was a damned hard memory to overcome. And at the same time, he knew he couldn't give up what he "needed" to do. Firefighting meant a lot to him.

The thought that she might leave and he'd never see her again made his chest burn. As they entered the Lonestar property, he wrapped his arm tighter around her waist.

They'd just started down the Lonestar drive when a black truck drove past them, kicking up dust behind its wheels as it sped along the driveway toward the house. Josh tensed. He recognized Jackson Riley's truck. His presence on the Lonestar only spelled trouble. "Hold on," he said in a low voice in Sabrina's ear, then kicked his heels in Ace's side so the horse would pick up his pace.

"Isn't that the officer from the hospital speaking to Nan? Officer O'Hara?" Sabrina asked as they approached the ranch.

"There they are," Nan called out from the porch as Josh stopped Ace and slid off his back. He kept an eye on Jackson as he wrapped the reins around the porch post, then helped Sabrina down.

The older man with salt and pepper hair climbed out of his truck and put on his black Stetson. "Hey, Josh." He nodded as he walked past them and stood at the bottom of the stairs staring up at Nan.

"What is it now, Jackson?" Nan asked in a curt tone.

"I came by to see what all the commotion was about last night." Jackson slid his gaze to the partially burned stables then back to her with a raised eyebrow. "I heard the fire trucks. What happened?"

"Someone attacked Miss Gentry last night and set the

stables on fire," Renee answered matter-of-factly. "Did you happen to see any strangers lurking around your property last night, Jackson?"

Jackson eyed Sabrina for a second, then shook his head. "Nah, tried to go to bed early, but all the blaring sirens woke me up."

Renee gave a firm nod, then turned to Sabrina. "How are you feeling today? Have you remembered anything?"

Sabrina touched her head and sighed. "I'm still a bit sore back there but, I'm sorry. I don't remember what happened."

"You were attacked here last night?" Jackson turned to them, his expression surprised.

Sabrina nodded.

"Who attacked you?" he asked.

She shook her head. "I don't know. It all happened so fast."

Putting out her hand, she smiled. "I'm sorry. I don't believe we've met. I'm Sabrina Gentry, here visiting my friend Elise."

Jackson stared at her for a second, his brown eyes assessing her before he grasped her hand and shook it. "Jackson Riley. My property neighbors the Lonestar land." Looking around, his brow furrowed as he shrugged his stocky shoulders and dug his hands deep in his back pockets. "Speaking of the Lonestar...when's Colt coming back?"

"He and Elise are due back tomorrow," Josh lied. He knew Jackson didn't have a sincere bone in his body. He didn't trust the man, nor did he want him to think the owner of the Lonestar was going to be absent for long.

Acknowledging Josh's answer with a grunt, Jackson looked at Sabrina once more, squinting against the bright afternoon sun. "You Elise's sister?"

Sabrina shook her head. "No. Just a college friend."

"As Josh said, Colt isn't here, Jackson. If you wish to speak with him, call ahead next time," Nan interrupted in a dry tone, letting him know she wanted him to leave.

While Jackson's lips tightened at the abrupt dismissal, Josh didn't bother holding back his grin at Nan's blatant dislike of the man. The older woman never was one to mince words.

Jackson stared at her for a second, then turned on his booted heel and headed for his truck. As he got in his vehicle and drove off, Nan mumbled, "Pain-in-the-ass old coot."

Renee nodded her understanding. "There's always one in the bunch."

Josh turned to Renee. "Did the escapee confess yet?"

She pulled a notepad out of her back pocket and said cryptically, "No. But I have a few more things to follow up on. By the way, what time is Colt due back tomorrow? I'd like to ask him a couple of questions."

"They aren't due back until day after tomorrow."

When she gave him a questioning look, he shrugged. "Their arrival time is none of Jackson's business."

She glanced at Sabrina as she pulled the pen from the spiral and jotted down a number. "If you remember anything, here's my cell. You can call me direct, okay?" When she finished, Renee tore off the piece of paper.

Sabrina stepped onto the porch to take it from her. "Thanks, I will, Officer O'Hara." As she started to shove it in her pocket, the note fell out of her hand and the wind blew it across the porch's floorboards. The paper skidded and came to a halt as it hit a railing, spun, then fell off the edge right behind the bushes that butted up against the porch.

When Josh started to go after the note for her, Sabrina said, "No, I'll get it." She quickly took the stairs down to the ground and went around to the front of the bushes. "It'll be easier to reach from under here, I think."

Stretching her arm under the thick hedge, she felt for the crumpled paper and stood up smiling as she shoved it in her jeans pocket. As she stared up at Renee on the porch, she grimaced. "I just wish I could help more."

Renee gave a rare smile. It made her look much younger than her thirty-one years. The kindhearted smile she gave Sabrina certainly didn't mesh with the tough investigative officer reputation she'd built over the years. But seeing her smile like that made Josh realize just how attractive she was. No wonder Dirk was pissed at him.

Renee walked down the stairs and put a hand on Sabrina's shoulder. "It'll come to you. Don't push it."

After Renee left, Josh and Sabrina had dinner with Nan. While they ate, Nan poked and prodded Josh several times, but Sabrina kept steering their conversation back to the Tanner brothers, Nan's favorite subject. Nan entertained them with stories of Colt and his brothers' antics. He knew some of these stories, but not all. Her tales made Josh grin; not only were they amusing, but he'd absorbed tons of future ribbing material.

Once the meal was over, he and Sabrina walked back outside on the porch. She put her small hand in his and looked up at him with a smile on her face. Damn, she tugged at his heart already.

"Ready to go home? Uh, I mean back to my house?" he asked. Why did it feel so easy to think of it as *their* home?

Without skipping a beat, she said, "Yes."

Yep, he was a goner. Now he needed to make sure she fell just as hard.

8

"So what's the deal with Nan's dislike of Jackson Riley?" Sabrina asked as Josh pulled himself up behind her on Ace's saddle.

He put his arm around her waist and nudged the horse into a walk back down the driveway toward Double K land. The warm Texas sun beat down on them, making her squint and appreciate the fact she'd braided her hair to keep it off her neck. He pulled her closer and said in a low tone, "I'm glad I didn't put a hat on you. Gives me an excuse to pull you close so my hat can offer some protection from the sun."

Sabrina chuckled at his excuse to hold her close, but appreciated the bit of shade his cowboy hat provided.

"In answer to your question, Jackson has spent a good portion of his life making Colt's family miserable for daring to own the land Jackson's father lost in a poker game."

"What land?" she asked, her curiosity piqued.

"Colt's land. Colt's uncle and dad bought the land from the winner of the poker game that Jackson's dad lost. That land is where the Lonestar ranch now stands. For years Jackson tried various ways to drive Colt's daddy and uncle apart; they each owned half of the land. Then there's the unexplained batches of bad water for the animals, maimed bulls and cattle, and several downed fences have occurred over the years."

"Um, I'm no rancher, but doesn't all that stuff happen sometimes on a ranch?"

She felt him shake his head behind her as he urged Ace into the woods back toward his property. "True, but not with the frequency that Colt has experienced it over the years. Did you know Elise inherited Colt's uncle's half of the Lonestar land when he died?"

Sabrina nodded. "Yeah, Elise told me Colt wasn't too happy when his uncle didn't leave the land to him as he'd promised he would."

Josh nodded. "I heard Jackson tried to buy the land from Elise, but then she met Colt. I'm sure their marriage annoyed the hell out of Jackson."

Sabrina snickered, then frowned as she considered Jackson Riley. Leaning back against Josh as Ace started to climb uphill, she asked, "Why hasn't Jackson been arrested for all that he's done?"

Josh snorted. "His last name should've been Wiley instead. For all the mischief he's caused, he's never been caught doing any of the things I mentioned. So it's just Colt's word against his."

"Man, that's got to suck for Colt." She sighed. "That's such a shame to have a neighbor like that. To never feel like he won't ever give up."

"He hasn't done much in a while," Josh mused. "Maybe he finally gave up once Elise married Colt. Because by doing so, she finally brought the two halves of ownership of the land back together after all these years."

Josh's hand slid up her waist, then grazed the side of her breast before his thumb traced her nipple lightly through her clothes. "Enough talk about Colt. There's only one man I want you thinkin' about," he said, his voice husky, insistent.

Sliding his thumb slowly back and forth across her nipple, he continued, "You see, there's only one woman on my mind, and I want to see her lying naked in my bed, her gorgeous black hair spread out over my pillows. That's my fantasy," he rasped, his aroused tone washing over her in a wave of tempting seduction. "Ready to make it a reality?"

Sabrina awoke the next morning to Josh staring at her. He was lying on his side with his head propped up in his hand. She let her gaze skim every part of his gorgeous body she could see. His messy blond hair and morning beard made him look sexier and even more like the bad boy she knew he could be.

"Morning," he said, his chest muscles flexing as he trailed a finger down her collarbone to the curve of her breast peeking out from underneath the white sheets and quilted comforter.

"Morning back." She rolled over in the bed to face him. Noticing the time on the clock, she said, "Oh my God, is it really ten thirty?"

Josh nodded, grinning. "Yeah, I've been up since dawn. Fed and exercised Ace and came back to bed to wait for you to wake up."

She wasn't sure what to say after the afternoon and evening they'd just spent together. She'd never been so physically in tune with another guy like she'd been with Josh. He seemed to have this ability to bring out the wild woman in her whenever he touched her. That's the only way she could explain how uninhibited she'd been with him.

"Sleep good?" He cupped the back of her head and pulled her up against his hard, naked chest as he leaned down and nuzzled her neck.

"Mmmm, hmmm," she responded, enjoying the smell of outdoors and leather mixed with his overall masculine scent. The rough feel of his whiskers on her neck and jaw made her heart race. "Though I am a bit sore from all the *extra* exercise I got yesterday."

"Daily exercise is good for your heart." He lifted his head and winked. "I recommend at least three times a day to keep you in shape."

She rubbed her hand across his scruff, eyes wide. "You mean three would be enough for you?"

He shook his head, an adamant expression on his face. "Uh-uh, darlin', that's just to get us start—"

The phone rang, interrupting him. Josh sighed and answered, his tone brisk, "Josh Kelly."

Sabrina half listened as she looked around his bedroom.

"I took the day off, Sam."

The surprisingly large room held very little furniture—a queen-sized bed with a mission-style wood headboard and a chest of drawers.

What she did like about the room was the extra-wide French doors that led to a brick patio facing the woods. She'd seen deer outside last night and a few rabbits. She loved being so close to nature.

"Okay, I'm on my way."

She turned to Josh with a questioning look as he hung up the phone.

"I'm sorry, Sabrina. There's a huge fire on the outskirts of town and they need all available firefighters on site."

As she watched Josh climb out of bed and make his way over to the walk-in closet, panic set in. Her heart raced, feeling as if it were going to burst from her chest. He couldn't have delivered more upsetting news to her. She rubbed her suddenly damp palms on the sheets and then gripped the cloth against her naked chest as she sat up.

"Do—do you really have to go?" She tried her best to keep the pleading out of her voice, but it seemed to creep in despite her efforts to suppress it.

Josh poked his head out of the closet, pulling on a white T-shirt. "Yeah. When the Chief calls, you know it's got to be important."

"But you did take the day off." She knew she must sound like the most selfish woman in the world while people's lives were in peril, but damn it, Josh's life was more important to her. Fear for his safety was uppermost in her mind. That combined with the realization of just how attached she'd grown to this man in such a short time hit her hard.

Josh came out of the closet pulling on a pair of firefighter pants, his brow furrowed as he looked at her. "I'm sorry I'm having to leave you. I'll be back as soon as I can."

He walked out of the room then came back in and handed her a phone. "Here's my cell. Keep it with you and call the number listed under Dirk if you need anything. He'll have his cell with him." He grinned as he touched her upturned chin. "And this phone even has a built-in GPS. That way, when I get back to the station I can track your whereabouts, so I can immediately know which room I'll be ravishing you in once I get home," he finished with a devilish smile.

She pushed a button on the cell phone and stared at the lit-up display. "Is the GPS really that precise?"

He chuckled, then rubbed his thumb along her bottom lip. "Nah, but I like to think about the possibilities of certain rooms we've yet to christen."

She pulled her bottom lip between her teeth, amazed by how easily he could excite her with just a touch. "Have you ever used that feature?"

He sat down on the bed and put on his shoes. "That phone was a gift from the guys at the firehouse. I'm...um... notorious for losing my cell phone." Glancing at her, his expression turned sheepish. "Keys I can seem to keep up with but my cells..." He trailed off, then shrugged. "The guys got me this cell phone for my birthday last year as a kind of joke. The truth is I actually have used the 'locator' feature several times. So far this year I haven't had to buy a new cell phone. Last year, I had to buy three. Gets expensive after a while."

Despite how upset she was, Sabrina managed a smile at this endearing look into Josh's foibles.

He leaned over and kissed her on her lips, lingering as if he really didn't want to go. Before she could grab his shoulder and beg him to stay, Josh pulled away, a regretful expression on his face.

He walked back over to his closet and grabbed his jacket. "Make yourself at home. TV remote's on the coffee table, and my laptop's yours if you need the internet for email and stuff. There's sandwich meat and cheese in the fridge, fruit, whatever you'd like for lunch. I'll be back before you know it."

It won't be soon enough, she thought as he walked out of the bedroom and left the house.

As soon as the door shut behind him, she climbed out of bed and headed for the shower. While the hard spray hammered down on her, she rubbed Josh's spice-scented soap over her body to try to stay focused on him and not where he was. But the only thoughts that filled her mind was losing her father and how difficult it had been for her to adjust to that loss.

She finished her shower and dried off, standing in front of the mirror. Wiping away the fog on the glass, she stared at her reflection. Fear and worry filled her deep green gaze.

How can you let yourself get so upset over this? She yanked the comb through her long, dark hair. *It's not like you and Josh are in a committed relationship*. For that matter, Josh certainly didn't say anything beyond this weekend together.

While she ran the hair dryer, she realized that the fact of the matter was she did care about Josh, cared what happened to him. She couldn't just stand by and watch the same thing happen to him that happened to her father even if they were just sleeping together.

Once she was dressed in a casual floral sundress, Sabrina smoothed the short skirt's cotton material across her thighs and walked into the living room. Standing in the center of the large open house, she heard every single sound the house made, from the creaking of a floorboard as she walked across it, to the ticking of the standup pendulum clock on the fireplace mantel. She opened the window, hoping the forest sounds would drain out the sounds of sheer emptiness she heard in the house everywhere she turned.

Hugging herself, Sabrina stared into the woods, wishing

she could talk to someone about her fears. Elise always knew how to make her feel better, but she had enough on her mind without Sabrina adding to the burden. Then it occurred to her exactly who she could talk to.

She walked back into the bedroom and picked up Josh's cell phone. She'd purposely left her own cell phone behind in Arizona. Otherwise she'd have never really *gone* on vacation from work. People always had a way of finding you if you had your cell phone with you.

Thinking about something happening to Josh had her stomach in painful knots. She really needed to talk to someone. "Please be home," she whispered as she dialed and waited for the phone to ring.

"Hello?"

"Hey Mom."

"Sabrina? Hi, honey. Hold a sec, let me get Taz in. Come on, boy. You've scared enough rabbits tonight."

Sabrina smiled, imagining their Border Collie chasing rabbits. The sound of a door shutting came across the line and her mom sighed. "Now I can talk. Where are you calling from? I don't recognize the number."

"I'm calling from Texas. I'm visiting my friend Elise on her ranch. Do you remember my roommate from college?"

"Oh yes. Such a sweet girl. How's she doing?"

Sabrina walked into the living room to look outside. "She's great. Recently married a cowboy."

"Good for her. Is he handsome?" her mother whispered in the phone.

Sabrina snickered. "Yes, and you should see him with Elise. She's his world."

"Your father was like that with me," her mother said wistfully. "Are you there on vacation?"

"Yes, I finally took some time off. Can you believe it?" She began pacing, working up her nerve to talk about things she'd never discussed with her mom.

"Well it's about time. You've been working so hard, dear. You don't sound very relaxed. Is everything all right?"

"I'm fine, Mom. Having a good time. I even met someone here."

"That's wonderful! But why do you sound so tense?"

Sabrina swallowed the lump in her throat and exhaled a deep breath. "There's just one problem. He's a firefighter."

"Oh, honey." Her mother released a sad sigh.

Sabrina clutched the phone close. "I know, I know, Mom. I would never have gone out with him if I'd known."

"Why?"

Sabrina stopped pacing, surprised by her mother's question. "Well, because of Dad," she answered, her voice shaking.

"Sabrina, I don't regret a single moment with your father. Even all the worrying I did was worth the time we had together. Don't let your fear keep you from getting to know this man. The really good ones are rare."

"Mom, he's fighting a fire as we speak, and I feel like I'm going to throw up. I just don't think I'm strong enough to handle this." She began pacing again, biting her thumb nail.

"How do you feel when you're with him?"

"What?"

"How does he make you feel?"

Sabrina stopped and stared at the carpet where they'd made love for the first time. "Wonderful. I've never felt this way about a man before. This was supposed to just be a fling, but I really like Josh. He's everything I've ever wanted, but—"

"If Josh makes you feel better than you've ever felt with anyone else, don't push him away. Give him a chance first, give the relationship a chance."

"But spending more time with him means I'll fall even deeper. I don't think I could handle worrying about him every time he goes to work."

"It won't happen overnight, Sabrina, but if you really care about Josh, your feelings for him will eventually overrule your worry of him being a firefighter. The fear of losing him in the line of duty may never go away, but if it means being with him or not being with him, that's a choice you'll have to decide on your own."

Sabrina squeezed her eyes shut and took a deep breath. "How did you do it, Mom?"

"I loved him, sweetheart. Plain and simple." Her mother was quiet for a second, then said, "I'm really glad you called. We've needed to talk about this for a long time. I'm just sorry you're not sitting in front of me so I could hug you right now. I'll always miss your father, Sabrina, but he died doing what he loved. Saving lives. I have no regrets. Not one. Make sure you live your life so you don't either, okay?"

Sabrina nodded. "I will, Mom. I love you."

"I love you too. Now go enjoy the rest of your vacation."

Sabrina felt a little better after she hung up with her mother. No, she wasn't a hundred percent but she could cope. Work was always a good outlet when one had too much time to ponder things. She hopped on Josh's laptop and logged into her email and checked it via the web. Yep, there were a hundred messages waiting to be answered.

She spent the next few hours responding to emails, only pausing to rummage through Josh's fridge and make herself some lunch. She couldn't believe how much work she'd gotten done. She'd been twice as efficient without people walking in her office to chat every so often. When her shoulders started to feel sore from sitting so long, Sabrina decided she'd worked long enough. She shut down the computer and looked at her watch.

Frowning as worry crowded her thoughts once more, she realized several hours had passed and she still hadn't heard from Josh. She moved to stand by the big picture window and stared out at the darkening sky and the trees blowing in the wind. A storm was brewing.

He could've called to reassure her he was okay and he didn't. Man, she was going to rail at him as soon as he walked in the door. Well, after she held him close and gave him a welcome home kiss. When she thought of something happening to him, her heart sped up and suddenly her rib cage felt too small for the wild beating that hammered against it. She put her hand on her chest, the sense of panic setting in as her breathing turned to short, choppy pants.

God, Josh better come home soon, or at this rate I'm going to pass out.

9

Sonofabitch, he ached all over. Josh stood under the hot stream of water in the firehouse's shower, washing away the sweat, soot and general grime from the fire. After they'd put the fire completely out, he didn't have a choice but to hitch a ride back to the fire station on the fire truck since his truck was gone. To save time, he'd driven his truck directly to the fire's location and parked away from the burning building. But while he did his civic duty, putting out a five-alarm fire, his damn truck had been towed.

Josh poured the fire station's antiseptic-smelling shampoo into his hair and hissed as the soap ran over the cut on his cheek. He thought about Sabrina while he lathered the suds. Hell, for that matter he'd thought about her all the way to the fire. Only while he fought the raging inferno was he able to disengage his thoughts about the woman he'd fallen in love with. Yeah, he'd admitted it to himself on his way to the fire, but how the hell was he going to convince her living with a fireman wasn't so bad?

Some shampoo got in his eye and without thinking he rubbed it hard, then winced, cursing Dirk for giving him the shiner earlier in the day.

"Sorry," his buddy had said as he elbowed him in the eye while they were pulling down the hoses. "See why it's important to have all your gear on. *Accidents* happen." Dirk had mock-scolded while Josh rubbed his injured eye.

"Screw you," Josh had grated.

"Nah, you already took care of that." Dirk tossed over his shoulder. Flashing him an unrepentant smile, Dirk had continued, "Now we're even."

Josh shut off the shower and after he toweled dry, he touched his sore eye. At least something good came from it. Since the tow truck place closed at three, he'd been able to guilt Dirk into giving him a lift back to the Double K after he took a shower.

"Hey, *little* man," Dirk smirked, purposefully glancing at Josh's naked lower body as he poked his head into the locker room. "You've got a phone call."

Josh grabbed his junk and faced his friend with an eat-shit-and-die smirk. "Bite me, Chavez." After he'd quickly dressed, he made his way to the front of the station house.

When he passed Dirk on his way to the phone, his buddy warned, nodding to his bruised eye, "I hope the reason she's calling you is strictly business or I'll have to give you a matching set."

"It's Renee?"

"None other," Dirk shot back in a dry tone before he walked away.

Josh picked up the receiver from the front desk. "Hello."

"Josh, hey, it's Renee. Listen, I need to get a hold of Colt. You know where he is, right?"

"What's this about?" he asked, his stomach tensing.

"I just need to talk to him, that's all."

He didn't like her evasiveness. "This has to do with your investigation, doesn't it? You still suspect Colt?"

When she didn't reply, he ground out, "You going to tell me or not?"

"No."

"Suddenly, my memory isn't so good. I'm hanging up now." He started to pull the phone away from his ear.

"Wait!"

"Yes?" he replied into the receiver.

"Time is of the essence here." She sighed. "I got a call yesterday from a concerned woman. She'd heard about the fire at the Lonestar Ranch and that someone had been in the fire. She said she wanted to make sure it wasn't Elise Tanner. She went on to say that she was out for dinner one night and overheard Colt tease his wife, saying that if he was ever really that hard up for cash, he could always bump her off and collect the life insurance money.

"Out of curiosity, I checked all the life insurance companies in town and a representative from the Oracle life insurance company confirmed Colt and Elise had recently taken out life insurance policies with their company."

Josh snorted. "So. They recently just got married. Makes sense to me."

"Maybe you're right and I've got it all twisted up, but Sabrina looks a lot like Elise, and from my notes the night of the accident, I know Elise leaving town was a last minute decision. The fact that the stables were locked from the outside while an unconscious woman lay in danger of burning to death inside sounds pretty intentional to me. If the attack on Sabrina was purposeful, it's possible she wasn't the intended target. Maybe whoever did this meant to attack Elise and not Sabrina. She did say she was hit from behind."

"Are you implying what I think you're implying?" he fairly yelled into the phone as his anger rose.

"Josh—"

"Colt is with Elise right now. You know that from our conversation yesterday."

"Wasn't he originally planning to be out of town, though? Nice alibi," Renee countered, leaving the implication dangling between them.

Josh took a couple of deep breaths. He might know Renee personally, but she was still an investigating officer and she took her job very seriously. He decided to go in another direction. "What about that escaped convict?"

"No dice. When we pressured him with an attempted murder charge on top of his other offenses, he finally confessed he'd broken into an empty house and stole some food and checks around the time Sabrina was attacked. The house he broke into was two miles away from the Tanner ranch. The homeowner confirmed the timing of the break-in because they arrived home to see someone running away from the house. There wasn't enough time for him to have been in both places at the same time."

Josh sighed, feeling like he'd been beat up twice today. He grudgingly gave her Colt's cell phone number. "You're way off base, Renee. Colt will set you straight."

When he hung up, he realized just how tense the ongoing investigation was making him. Sabrina meant everything to him. The need to be by her side was all he wanted right now. "Dirk, we've got to go!"

JOSH LEFT Ace in his stable while he dashed through the pouring rain to his porch. He'd rub his horse down after he saw Sabrina. He had to see her and hold her close.

Opening the door, he walked inside and quickly surveyed his place. Relief washed over him when his gaze snagged on Sabrina curled up in the window seat, leaning against the glass. He shut the door against the gusting wind then turned, tossing his hat on the chair and started to say, "Man it's raining like crazy out there—" when he was jolted back a step as Sabrina launched herself into his arms.

As she squeezed his neck tight and wrapped her legs around his waist, he held her close and closed his eyes, inhaling her sweet smell.

"Thank God you're okay," she breathed out, kissing his cheek, then his jaw before pressing her lips to his mouth.

Josh wrapped his arms around her and kissed her back, grinning. "Now that's a hell of a welcome home. I could get used to this."

Sabrina tensed in his arms and lowered her legs to the ground. Still holding on to him, she put her head on his chest and asked in a worried voice, "It's been hours. Why didn't you call me to let me know you were okay?"

His brow furrowed. "What do you mean?' Didn't you get my text?"

She glanced up at him with a confused look. "What message?"

Spying his cell phone on the coffee table, he let her go and picked it up. He frowned at the settings for a second, then his eyebrows shot up. "That's right. I forgot I left it on vibrate mode. You wouldn't have heard it ping with my text."

He set down the phone as she approached, saying in a suggestive tone, "I logged on when we got back and sent a message to my cell, asking you to meet me in the stables. That's one place we hadn't christened yet. Plus, I just wanted you to know I was thinking about you," he finished with a wink as he faced her.

"Ohmigod, look at your eye and that gash on your cheek! What happened?" she asked, eyes wide.

"The cut was dumb luck at the fire and the black eye was Dirk deciding I needed a little payback for my transgressions against him," he joked. When he saw all the color drain from her face, he reached for her. "What's wrong, Sabrina?"

She dodged his hand and backed away saying to herself, her gaze glazed over, "I thought I could handle...but I just can't."

"Sabrina?" Before he could reach her, she'd turned on her bare feet and dashed to the front door. Pulling it open, she ran out into the pouring rain.

"Sabrina!" he called out again and took off after her.

SABRINA'S HEART thundered as she ran down the steps. The pouring rain immediately soaked her dress through, but she kept running. Her heart hurt as if someone had tried to rip it from her chest. She couldn't put herself through another loss. Losing her father was enough. Not another person she'd come to care for, especially on such a deeply connected level. Her mother was much stronger than her. She knew it was crazy to run out into the rain, but she just needed to get the hell out of there. If she reacted this way to something as simple as a black eye and the ragged cut on his face... God, she felt so sick to her stomach.

She fought through the cramps gripping her belly as she heard Josh call her name from the porch. Thankful she was barefoot, she dug her toes in the grass and bolted toward the woods. Twenty-five feet. If she could just get there, she could have some time to herself. Get away from Josh and every deep-seated emotion his handsome face and endearing ways caused to churn within her.

Sabrina's heart broke at the realization of just how much she cared for Josh. Warm tears streamed down her face only to be washed away by the unrelenting cool rain.

Her breathing turned choppy and her lungs felt like they were on fire as she pushed herself to the limit to get to her destination as fast as she possibly could. Josh's heavy footfalls sounded not far behind her. The noise both comforted and scared her.

When she was within ten feet of the entrance to the woods, she felt a hand around her ankle and she went down, hard on her stomach.

Sobbing, she clawed at the grass, trying to free her ankle from Josh's grasp, but he was too fast and before she could move another inch, he'd rolled her over on her back and had pinned her to the ground with his body.

"No," she wailed and swung her arm, doing her best to free herself from his touch, his attentiveness, his damned sexy heat. Her elbow accidentally hit his jaw, causing his head to snap sideways.

"Sonofabitch, Brina!" he hissed out as he grabbed her arms. Slamming them to the ground above her head, his teal gaze narrowed on her. "Why are you running and why the hell are you trying to break my jaw?"

"I'm sorry, Josh. I didn't mean to hit you," she replied, feeling suddenly hemmed in and vulnerable, her heart out there flailing in the wind. "Let me up," she panted, resuming her struggles as she bucked to get him off of her. She needed to get away from him before she had a complete breakdown.

"You're not going anywhere until you tell me what's wrong." Josh pressed his hips to hers, holding her firmly to the ground. Her heart raced at his deep concern for her, while at the same time she couldn't mistake the hard flesh that nudged against her.

She jerked a surprised gaze his way and he ground out, "Hell yeah, I still want you even when we're fighting...over God knows what! What's wrong?" he asked again, a look of utter confusion and frustration crossing his face.

"I guess I need some space," she mumbled as she looked away from him, her chest constricting.

Josh cupped the back of her head, turning her to face him once more. Water ran in rivulets down the muscle ticcing in his jaw as his piercing gaze met hers, willing her to listen. "Why? So you can run from us? Run from what you know is right?"

She blinked away the pouring rain, thankful the pounding water made it harder for her to meet his intense gaze.

His grip on her head tightened as he rasped out, "I love you, Sabrina. I won't let you shut me out."

Surprise jolted through her at his words. Sabrina raised her hand to hold on to his wrist. Her heart hammered out of control, in complete disregard for her earlier worries over her feelings for Josh. "Wha-what did you just say?"

His expression softened and he let go of her arm, then rubbed his thumbs along her jawline, saying in a rough voice, "I said I'm hopelessly, madly, deeply in love with you."

Emotions swirled within her...emotions she hadn't acknowledged and refused to identify. She didn't know how to respond to his declaration—to tell him his mere touch made her melt like no other man's did, but she couldn't handle being with a fireman.

"Josh, I—"

Josh didn't give her a chance to reply. He pulled her close and covered her mouth with his lips, his kiss tender yet dominant.

As his tongue brushed against hers, Sabrina wondered why all rational thoughts fled her brain every time the man's lips met hers. She kissed him back with all the passion she felt but couldn't express in words.

Thunder rumbled overhead, then lightning slashed, splintering the dark sky above them.

Josh broke their kiss, glancing up at the sky. He quickly pulled her to her feet, saying as he put his arm around her waist, "That lightning was a little too close for comfort. Come on, we're closer to the stables. We'll wait out the storm there."

Sabrina followed him inside the structure, the smell of rain, hay, horseflesh, and the faint smell of manure assailing her nostrils.

Ace neighed as Josh shut the stable doors against the driving rain. Sabrina smiled and walked over to calm the horse, noting all the empty stalls. Rubbing her hand down the animal's neck, she spoke to him in a soothing tone, "It's okay, boy. We're here to wait out the storm with you."

The horse snorted and pawed the ground as if pleased. She smiled as she patted his neck.

"You've got the touch with horses," Josh commented right behind her as he pressed his chest against her back.

"Not like you do," she said as his heat radiated, seeping into her pores and warming her, despite the wet clothes on his body. She inwardly acknowledged her desire to push thoughts of walking away from Josh out of her mind for the time being. Why did he have to feel so right standing behind her, protecting her, loving her and damn it, seeming to understand her better than she understood herself?

"As much as you love horses, I'm surprised you don't have more on your own land. You've certainly got the room for them," she said, glancing at the empty stalls as she tried to get her tumultuous emotions under control.

"Right now I work too many hours to give them the attention they would need."

Josh pushed her wet hair out of the way, then trailed his lips down her throat. "Hmmm, the way you smell turns me on," he ground out as he nipped at her neck.

Heated and hungry were the only two words she could think of to describe the intensity in his voice. And the sound caused her body to react in swift unadulterated arousal. Her nipples hardened, her stomach tensed and her sex pulsed while she turned to face him with bated breath. Josh had taken off his shirt and now stood in front of her in his wet jeans. His biceps flexed while he kept his hands down by his sides—as if it took supreme effort to do so.

His jaw muscle flexed as he reached out and ran his finger

across a nipple through her thin dress. Soaking wet, the material clung to her skin, and without a bra, the combination did nothing to hide her pink nipples underneath.

"I've never seen a more beautiful sight in my life," he whispered as he clasped her around her upper back and pulled her to him to clamp his mouth over the hardened bud he'd just touched.

Sabrina arched her back and dug her fingers into his shoulders as he bit down on the cloth-covered dark pink bud, then sucked it into his mouth.

Sliding his thigh between hers, he moved his lips to her jaw and slowly unzipped the zipper on the back of her dress. The distinctive sound only seemed to accentuate the heated silence in the stables.

As Josh's lips found hers once more, he pushed the straps of her sundress down her arms, then to her waist.

While she shrugged out of her dress, Josh rubbed his thumbs across the taut peaks. The hard-working, rough surface of his fingers grazing across her sensitive nipples distracted her, setting her on a ragged edge.

Sabrina moved close to his chest and wrapped her arms around his neck, purposefully rubbing her breasts against the hard surface. The warm, taut skin stretched over his well-defined muscles pressing against her only made her want more. Clasping his neck tight, she lifted herself and wrapped her legs around his waist.

Josh grabbed her rear and squeezed while his teal green gaze seemed to penetrate straight to her soul. "I want to be inside you so bad I can't think straight."

Smiling, she threaded her fingers through his thick, wet hair and kissed him.

Josh returned her kiss, his tongue stroking deep inside until their breathing turned choppy. He set her down beside Ace, his voice tight. "Turn around."

Excited by this barely controlled side of Josh, Sabrina turned around.

When Josh lifted her hands and clasped them around the horse's saddle horn, she wondered what he was doing. She had to elevate her heels off the ground a bit to get a full grip. Expecting Josh to slide her underwear down, she was surprised when he slowly unwound Ace's reins from the post. As he began to wind the leather straps around her hands on the saddle, her heart rate kicked up to a thunderous rhythm.

"What are you doing?" She glanced up at him nervously as he leaned over her to complete his task. She'd tried to keep her tone calm, even though she felt far from it.

After he'd cinched the reins into a knot around her hands, Josh only gave her a wicked smile before he patted Ace on the neck and commanded, "Hold boy."

"Josh!" she began, getting a bit anxious. "I'm not—"

He pressed his back to hers once more, then cupped her breasts in his hands while he kissed her neck and said, "Shhh, baby." Aroused tension filled the air as he slid a hand down her hip. then gave a hard tug on her underwear, ripping the wispy material right off her body.

Goose bumps formed on her arms and her nipples tightened. His fierceness lit her on fire. She couldn't help but squirm when he skimmed his fingers up her spine and said in a knowing tone, "You like it when you don't have all the control, don't you." It wasn't a question. It was an assured statement.

She swallowed back her excitement when she felt his knuckles against her ass as he unbuttoned his pants. All the blood in her body rolled straight to her core in a near painful rush.

"I've seen the way you react when I've held your arms while I thrust inside you. It turns you on."

In the dimness, Sabrina stared at the stable's far wall, not wanting to admit he was right. Hell, for that matter, she didn't even know if he was right. "No, I—"

Josh clasped her hips and rasped against her ear as he nudged her stance further apart with a booted foot. "I want to feel every part of you, Brina. Do I need a condom?" he asked and she felt the press of his erection just outside her wet entrance.

She shook her head. "No, I'm on the pill. Trust goes both ways—"

He entered her as she spoke, a swift, hard, deep thrust. The decadent sensation of being taken from behind caused her to scream out in fulfilled satisfaction. The fact she didn't have a sure-footed hold while Josh had to bend his knees slightly to accommodate the differences in their heights made her feel protected and cherished. Her suspended-in-the-air position where their bodies joined felt seductively erotic and so very intimate.

Josh stayed buried deep within her as he moved his hands to cup her breasts. Rolling her nipples between his fingers, he applied just the right amount of pressure. Sabrina put her chin to her chest, her breath coming in tiny pants.

"I can touch you anywhere I want," he said as he slid his palm slowly down her stomach. Once he'd reached the tiny triangle of hair between her legs, he rubbed a finger through it and against her sensitized skin until he found her clit. Circling the hard bit of skin, he finished with a satisfied tone, "And all you can do is come."

As much as she loved what he was doing to her body, Sabrina couldn't help but give him some of his own medicine. "If my hands weren't tied, I'd grab that nice ass of yours and pull you deeper," she taunted.

Josh groaned and gripped her hips. Tilting her pelvis forward slightly he ground his hips against hers, thrusting upward even deeper. "Like this?"

Sabrina could've sworn she saw stars with his aggressive move, but she was determined to let him know how much control she still had. "No, like this," she said, clenching her inner muscles to contract her walls around his cock.

He tensed behind her, then lowered his head to her shoulder. He didn't move or say a word. All she could hear was his shallow breathing and the rain hammering the roof above their heads. Seconds ticked by as she waited for him to move.

Then his fingers flexed on her hips, letting her know...she'd gotten to him.

WITH HER LAST ACTION, Sabrina had made him literally shudder and his knees almost give way. Despite his wet skin, his body broke out in a heated sweat. Josh had a hard time keeping his cool. He'd never felt such bone-deep, body-jarring sensations with anyone else, not like he did with Sabrina. Loving someone as fiercely as he loved her must heighten and intensify the pleasure. He wanted to take his time with her, bring her to peak with his hands first, but seeing her gorgeous naked body like this and discovering more about her responsive nature...damn, he was revved. It was taking all his willpower not to just fuck her senseless like he wanted to.

Finally he gritted out, "I wanted this to last, to draw it out..." He stopped speaking and inhaled and exhaled to keep it together. "I've never wanted to just *take* someone so bad in my life."

She sucked in her breath, then arched her spine, pushing herself against him. "Go for it, cowboy. I'm more than ready to *take* all you're willing to give."

Josh clenched his jaw as her warm body pressed further into his, as if she somehow hoped to physically fuse her body with him. He'd never felt more connected to another person and the thought rocked him deeply. The softness of her skin, her sweet ass rubbing against him, the arousing smell of sex all around them, hell yeah, she was ready. He held her hips while he withdrew and slammed back inside.

As pleasurable sensations ricocheted throughout his body, he pulled out and thrust in once more, clenching his jaw at the coiled sexual buildup slamming into his groin.

He dropped one hand from her hip to rub her clit while he slid inside her again, this time holding himself deep. When she screamed out and he felt her warm core contracting around his cock, fisting him in a tight glove of renewed wetness, he groaned in pent-up relief.

"Brina," he breathed out as he came, rocking his hips as his entire frame shook with a fire that burned straight down to his toes. No other sexual partner's orgasm had caused such a heightened, satisfying response within him, a response that went way beyond a physical level.

After they both stopped moving, their breathing still ragged, he cupped her breasts and leaned his chest flush against her back to press a soft kiss to her shoulder. "I'm never letting you go."

"Well, eventually you'll have to," she giggled as she tugged on the reins around her hands.

He clasped her butt cheeks and squeezed. "Or I could put you up on the saddle just as you are, tied and naked, and give you a ride to the house."

You wouldn't dare!" She began to tug on her bonds.

"Why bother putting your clothes back on, darlin'? They're soaking wet. Plus, you'll just end up without them again once I get you inside," he finished as he reached over her and untied the reins.

"And here I thought taking off my clothes and ripping my underwear from my body was half the fun," she teased as she cast him a saucy grin over her shoulder.

"Never doubt it." Freeing her, he turned her in his arms and kissed her nose. "The storm's fury seems to be letting up. We'd better get you into some dry clothes."

10

Sabrina lay in Josh's bed with his arms wrapped around her as they listened to the rain outside. They'd had a sexually charged dinner, amid many interruptions as Josh dabbed beef gravy on her nose just so he could kiss if off, which led to a heated kiss and finally they'd ended up in his bedroom.

The room was completely dark except for the occasional flash of lightning that lit up the entire room. Josh created a soothing rhythm as he ran his fingers through her hair from her scalp to the ends and then back again.

She moaned and said without conscious thought, "I could get used to this."

Josh never stopped stroking her hair as he replied, "Then why not make this a permanent deal? Stay in Texas with me, Sabrina."

Sabrina jerked her gaze to his in the dark, thankful for the brief flash of lightning that lit up his face so she knew for sure he wasn't joking. A sincere expression greeted her questioning look before the room doused in darkness once more. She'd assumed he'd told her he loved her in the heat of the moment. Even though it had made her heart jerk to hear the words, she wasn't sure he'd meant it in a committed way.

"We—we barely know each other," she argued, trying to keep a calm on her rioting senses and thudding heart. *He wanted her to stay permanently*?

Josh shifted, pulling her underneath him, his response calm, assured, "I've waited a lifetime to feel the way I do when I'm with you, Brina. God knows I've had some inner demons to face along the way, but since you've come into my life, I've been able to find a sense of balance I'd never been able to before. I'm not just going to let you go."

Surprised by his cryptic comment about his past and thrilled by his possessive, protective nature, her heart sank that she'd have to set him straight. She should've done so when he first told her he loved her. Putting her hands on his chest, she started to reply, "Josh, I'm here for now but—"

The phone rang, interrupting her. "Who the hell could be calling at this hour?" Josh cursed at the interruption as he picked up the cordless phone from its receiver on his nightstand.

"Hello?"

Sabrina waited, her entire body tensed at the possibility the phone call meant Josh would have to go fight yet another fire.

"Yeah, see you then. Thanks."

Josh hung up the phone and turned back to her, answering her unspoken question. "That was Dirk calling to tell me when he planned to pick me up."

"Pick you up? Not to fight another fire?" she asked, her voice unconsciously going up an octave.

Josh rolled over and pulled her across his chest. His hands flexed as he rubbed up and down her arms. "I meant, pick *us* up and no, there's no fire this time. I promise."

"Pick us up?" she repeated, curious as to where they were going.

"Yeah, my truck got towed yesterday while I was fighting that fire. Tomorrow morning Dirk's going to take us to get it."

He ran his hand up her shoulder and under her hair to cup the back of her neck. Rubbing his thumb across her jaw and throat, he said, "And yes, I meant us. I don't want you out of my sight any longer than necessary. Your memory could come back at any time. By my side is where you belong."

Warmed by how protective he sounded, she said, "I'm sure you can handle it without me."

Josh sighed. "I was hoping to avoid telling you this...to keep you from worrying, but the escaped prisoner has an alibi. It seems he was busy breaking and entering in another house while you were attacked. So that means whoever attacked you is still out there.

"At this point, your attacker has to know by now that you didn't die in that fire, which could make you a target. He doesn't know you don't remember what happened to you. And since the details are still fuzzy to you, for all you know, you might have seen his face and could identify him."

"Oh God, I hadn't thought of that." Fear raced through her at the possibility Josh could be right. "Okay, I'll go with you tomorrow."

"After we pick up my truck, I'll give Colt a call. I'm hoping he was able to get Renee off his back."

"What are you talking about?" She frowned at him, confused.

"Renee's checking 'all angles' on the stable fire and your attack. She received a phone call from a 'concerned citizen' about the attack at the Tanner ranch. The lady who called said she overheard Colt tease Elise at dinner that if he were really in dire need for money, he could just bump her off and collect the life insurance money."

"That's crazy!" Pure outrage filled her that anyone would even consider Colt a suspect. "Anyway, *I* was attacked, not Elise."

"Yeah, but everyone agrees you and Elise could easily be mistaken for each other and you *were* attacked at night, so for all those reasons, Renee is looking into it." His arms around her tightened before he continued, "Of course, I don't agree with it. I'm sure Colt will set her straight."

Once they'd finished discussing the case and the silence stretched out between them, Sabrina felt the tension build in Josh's chest and arms, as if he were a tightly coiled spring, ready to snap. Wondering what current thoughts would cause him to tense up, her own stomach began to knot in response.

Why couldn't she pretend he'd never said, "I love you" or asked her to stay in Texas?

"Are you planning to answer my question?" he finally spoke, his voice tight as he placed his hands on her arms once more.

She let out a sigh and replied, "I'm sorry, Josh. There can't be more between us. I can't stay." *I'm just not strong enough.*

His hands gripped her arms in a firm hold. "Why?"

"As I said, we barely know each other. Plus I work in Arizona—"

"Bullshit! You told me how much work you got done today working at home. I'll bet your job could be done anywhere. What you and I share is indescribable, Brina. I don't want to just walk away from that. Give it to me straight or not at all," he said in a clipped tone.

She stiffened in response to his anger. "Fine. You want it straight? I can't deal with you being a fireman. That's why I ran earlier. I felt physically ill while you were gone all day today, Josh. Then seeing you'd gotten hurt today, even the tiniest bit, threw me over the edge. I can't go through that every day, hoping you won't end up like my dad."

"That was just a scratch, baby," he cajoled. When she didn't respond, he said in a subdued voice, "You asked me about Nick the other night. He was my childhood friend. That picture you saw was taken the day we'd played all day long, pretending to be a fireman and a police officer. That day he told me he planned to be a cop, and he said I should be the firefighter I'd dressed as, since I was the best fire starter and extinguisher on the planet." Josh chuckled fondly before his tone turned melancholy once more.

"We'd planned to meet in our fort the next day, but Nick never made it. His house caught on fire that night, killing Nick and his entire family. A previous lightning strike weakening the wiring might've been the culprit. The report was never conclusive as to what caused the fire."

Sabrina's heart contracted for how Josh lost his childhood friend. She laid her head on his chest and listened as he took a deep, steadying breath and finished his tale.

"Ever since then, I've wanted to be a firefighter." He lifted his shoulders, shrugging underneath her. "I know it's irrational, but I guess deep down every time I fight a fire, I'm fighting that fire I never could for Nick, since I couldn't be there for him when he needed me the most."

"Is that why you carry Nick's gun too?" she asked quietly.

He didn't speak for a second. "Noticed that, did you? Nick's dad bought those guns, and Nick gave me the other one. We practiced shooting all the time. Nick finally outshot me that day the picture was taken. He'd claimed that being a crack shot proved he'd be a hero one day. He never got to be that hero, so yeah, I guess I carry his gun to keep a part of him with me."

She blinked back hot tears and felt the stirrings of deep love and appreciation tug on her heart. Sabrina fought the emotion that flooded her body. How, in good conscience, could she ever ask him to give up firefighting after that sad story? She couldn't. "See what I mean. Fires cause nothing but pain and heartache."

He hooked her chin and turned her face toward his. The sky lit up once more and Sabrina briefly saw his down-turned eyebrows and serious expression. "I'm working on trying not to see an invisible ghost in every fire I fight or setting unrealistic expectations for myself, but..." He paused and rubbed his thumb across her chin. "The need to fight fires will always burn within me, Sabrina. I can't explain it any better than that."

"Just as my own experiences affect the decisions I make," she replied. "After losing my father the way I did, I vowed I would never have a relationship with a firefighter."

"I could just as easily die in a car accident tomorrow," he countered.

He was right, but she knew her own mind well enough. She'd make herself sick with worry every time he walked out the door, regardless of how many valid rebuttals he threw her way. "Yes, you could," she replied, her heart sad. "But being a firefighter, the nature of the risks you take are beyond everyday life stuff. They're beyond what I know I can handle."

"So that's it? In a few days, you'll just walk away from me, from us, as if we'd never met, never connected, never meant more to each other than spectacular fuck partners?"

She gulped at how callous and cold he made her sound. She knew he was hurt by her rejection. Hearing that hurt in his gruff tone was bad enough. She was thankful for the darkness so she didn't have to see his teal gaze shift to a deep sea green as it churned with turmoil.

Slowly she nodded, knowing he could feel her answer since his hand was still on her chin. "I will."

He swiftly flipped her over on her back, pulling her arms above her head as he thrust his thigh between hers. "Then I have very little time left to convince you that staying with me is far preferable than living without me," he said in a determined voice.

"Josh, I know you're upset—"

"I don't want your sympathy, Brina." He pressed his erection against her entrance. "I want *this* to mean more," he ground out as he thrust deep.

Sabrina screamed at the satisfying completeness she felt when he was seated inside her—every time she felt that way, damn him. Sad tears streamed down her face as he began to move within her in measured, deliberately slow, tantalizing strokes. Her heart raced and desire swirled in her belly as her body temperature rose.

When she moaned in ecstasy, his breathing sawed in and out, but his tone remained unwavering, determined. "I know I have your body, but I won't give up until I have your heart and soul too."

His vow stabbed at her, making their lovemaking the most bittersweet and emotionally intense she'd experienced with him. His heartfelt words, his knowing touch, the way they perfectly moved in tune with one another...it all broke her heart. Sabrina silently acknowledged to herself that Josh did have her body. He even had her heart, but she couldn't allow her soul to burn up in that white-blue flame only he seemed to be able to ignite within her.

I SIT in the wooden mission-style chair a few feet away from the front door. Mom doesn't like that I've taken it from the kitchen table, but I don't care. My hands are folded in my lap and I bite my lower lip, waiting.

Mom tries to lure me away with ice cream and cookies like she did when I was little, but I shake my head even though my belly is growling. I never look away from the door.

Dad's coming home soon. He'll burst through the door all sweaty and smelling of smoke, his face streaked with soot. He'll say he came straight from work just to pull me into a bear hug.

My brothers try to engage me in conversation, but I tune them out, staying focused. The only time I look away is to glance at the clock on the mantel in the living room. It's seven. Why isn't he home yet?

"Sabrina, your father's not coming." Mom touches my shoulder. Why does she sound sad?

I want to look at her, but I'm afraid what I'll see on her face.

"He's never coming home, sweetie," she says, her voice cracking. "I'm sorry."

I shake my head in adamant jerks and press my lips together. My back aches and my butt hurts from sitting so long, but I refuse to move. "He's coming, Mom," I say, even though my voice shakes.

"He's gone, Sabrina," my brother Jason says. "You need to move on. Let him go."

"No, he's not gone!" I scream. I want to tear my gaze away so I can challenge him, prove him wrong, but I don't. "Dad's coming home!" I never got to say goodbye. Never got to hug him once more. He can't be gone. I won't let him be.

"He died, little Bri," my oldest brother Thomas says. He places his big hand on top of my head to comfort me. "We all miss him."

I close my eyes and the action pushes my tears down my cheeks. Then I blink them open and snap my aching spine straight again, dashing the wetness from my cheeks. "No. He's coming!"

My eyes burn from staring so long without blinking, but finally the feel of my brother's hand on my head fades away.

I exhale a sigh of relief. They don't believe like I do.

Then suddenly my chair is being tugged away from the door. I try, but I can't get up. I grab onto the seat and scream my fury as I'm pulled further and further away and the door grows smaller and smaller until I can no longer see it.

"Sabrina!" A man's worried voice penetrates my mind. Why does it sound familiar?

Sabrina blinked in the darkness. She panted through the disorientation until tender lips pressed against her temple. "It's just a nightmare, baby." Josh pulled her against his sleep-warmed chest, gathering her close as he laid them back down in his bed. "You were screaming, 'Take me back,' over and over." He pushed her hair away from her face and turned her toward him.

Sabrina swallowed several times to calm herself. She hadn't had that dream in a long time. "I'm sorry," she mumbled into his chest.

He lifted her chin. "You're still trembling. Talk to me about it. Maybe it'll help."

She appreciated his desire to make her feel better. Maybe it was because it was dark and she couldn't see his face, or maybe it was because it bothered her that this dream resurfaced when she thought she'd shut that door in her life, but whatever the reason, she told Josh about her dream when she'd never told anyone before, not even her family.

When she stopped talking, she was surprised tears were streaming down her cheeks. "I used to dream it every night for a while." She sniffled, then sighed. "But I haven't had it in a very long time." Josh brushed her tears away with his thumbs and pulled her close to press a kiss to her forehead. "I'm sorry, Sabrina, so sorry."

She laid her head on his chest. "You have nothing to be sorry for. It was just a dream."

JOSH STROKED Sabrina's hair until she fell back asleep. As she told him about her dream, a heavy ache filled his chest. Whether she realized it or not, he was the reason she'd had that dream. Now, her freaking out on him when he came home late from fighting that fire made complete sense. How would they ever get past this? Sabrina's demons were just as deeply ingrained as his.

When she sighed in her sleep and started to roll away, he turned on his side and pulled her back, spooning her against his chest. Kissing the back of her head, he slid a leg between hers and wrapped his arm around her waist. He didn't want her leaving his side, not even while she slept. He buried his nose in her hair and inhaled deeply. He'd find a way to make this work. She was too important to him.

11

The next morning, Sabrina and Josh shared a quiet breakfast of bacon and pancakes, thanks to Josh's fabulous cooking. Their mutual silence was almost as if they didn't want to break the peaceful spell that had settled over them. But Sabrina saw the heat in his gorgeous teal eyes every time Josh looked at her across the table. It was as if he thought he could *will* her to say, "Yes, I'll stay."

When they were done with their meal, he stood then walked around the table to hold his hand out to her. He looked so sexy in his black T-shirt, faded jeans and black cowboy boots. Even the bruised black eye and cut on his cheek worked in his favor, enhancing his rugged good looks. All this "certified" cowboy was missing was his Stetson, but she was glad he didn't have one on at the moment, because it would only hide his sexy blond hair. She really loved running her fingers through those thick wavy locks.

She put her hand in his and allowed him to pull her into his arms. As she wrapped her arms around his waist, she'd never felt more secure and loved than she did when Josh's strong arms surrounded her. The spicy aroma of his aftershave teased her nostrils and she buried her nose in his shirt, enjoying the smells of laundry soap, aftershave and all male.

"Look at me," he said quietly.

Sabrina lifted her chin and elevated her gaze to meet his serious one. He searched her face before he spoke. "I meant what I said last night. I love you too much to let you go."

She closed her eyes, unable to meet his gaze. When he laid a gentle kiss on each eyelid, she let out a tortured sob. The man just made her heart turn to sheer mush and her knees literally threaten to give out. Good thing he had her locked in a bear hug or she'd be a melted puddle on the floor at his feet.

He gave a low laugh. "I'd just pick you up and make you melt all over again."

Her eyes flew open and heat rode up her cheeks. "Did I just say that out loud?"

"Yes, you did," came his satisfied reply, amusement dancing in his eyes. He slid his hands down to cup her rear, pulling her fully against his body. "And don't think for one minute I'll let you forget it, darlin'. I'll use every weapon in my arsenal when it comes to convincing you that you belong with me."

The ruthless look in his gaze belied the lightheartedness in his tone. Sabrina resisted the shiver that threatened to shimmy up her spine at the promise in his eyes.

A distinctive beep-beep sound outside interrupted the arc of sexual energy and dual displays of willpower that seemed to flow unspoken between them.

Josh frowned, then walked over to open the door. Sabrina

followed him to see Dirk pulling his helmet off as he sat on his motorcycle, a wide grin on his face.

"Well, I'll be damned." Dirk's eyes lit up. "Aren't you just the luckiest dog around?" he said to Josh as he stared at Sabrina standing next to his friend. Nodding to her, he grinned, "Hello again, gorgeous."

"Hi, Dirk," she replied and held back a grin when Josh jerked his gaze to her, jealousy and surprise evident on his face.

Stepping slightly in front of her, Josh said, "You two know each other?"

She rolled her eyes at his blatant attempt to shield her from Dirk's view, then stepped around him onto the porch. "Dirk gave me a ride to the Lonestar when I first arrived in Boone."

"Got your rental car?" Dirk asked.

She nodded. "Yep, the very next day. Then Elise convinced me to return it. Turns out she was right. I haven't needed it. Thanks again for your help."

Josh stepped into place beside her on the porch, his stance tense. "Why did you bring your bike?" he asked Dirk. "I wanted Sabrina to go with me to get my truck."

"Might've helped if you had mentioned that bit of information," Dirk shot back. "I just thought it'd be fun to take my bike up the hills to get to your place."

Sensing the tension flowing between the men, Sabrina jumped in, "It's okay, Josh. Didn't you say the towing place wasn't that far away? I'll wait here for you to get back. No big deal."

He turned a concerned gaze her way. "I don't want to leave you alone."

"No one even knows where I am. Remember, we kept it a secret," she replied, winking.

Sighing, Josh nodded reluctantly, then walked inside to retrieve his keys and his wallet. When he came back out, he said, "I'll be back in a half hour."

She smiled up at him as he bent to kiss her.

"Let's go, stud." Dirk tossed a spare helmet Josh's way as he came down the stairs.

Once Josh put his helmet on and got on behind him, Dirk revved the motorcycle's engine and turned the bike around. Before he left, Dirk gave Sabrina a rakish grin. "Don't worry, he'll be back in record time."

"I'd prefer in one piece," she called after the loud motorcycle as the men took off.

After Josh left, she walked inside and cleaned their breakfast dishes. Picking up the remote, she clicked on the TV for background noise as she continued to scan the house for something to do to occupy her time. When her gaze landed on his laptop sitting on the desk, she decided to see if she had any responses to the emails she'd sent out yesterday.

She sat down at the desk and watched the last few minutes of an old sitcom rerun while she waited for his computer to boot up. Sifting through her email, she found a few that needed immediate attention and once she'd responded to those mails, her gaze was drawn to the news update that flashed across the screen.

Eddie Clayton, the escaped convict who was recently apprehended after four hours of freedom, was just transferred to a maximum security prison today. He awaits his trial where additional sentencing will be given for his latest crimes.

When the picture of the convict popped up on the TV screen, recognition dawned and suddenly that night came flooding back to her. She'd watched the news report, saw the convict's photo, heard the noise outside, then picked up the lantern and...and...there was a note and she'd set it down on the railing when she picked up the lantern. What did it say? Damn, why couldn't she remember more?

Maybe if she could find that note, it would jog the rest of her memory. Grabbing Josh's cell phone, she quickly dialed the Tanners' residence.

"Hello?" a woman answered.

"Nan? Hi, it's Sabrina. A bit of my memory has just come back, but I'm hoping you can help me."

"Oh, that's great news! I'd be glad to help if I can. What can I do?"

"The night I was attacked, someone left a lantern sitting on top of a note on the porch. I remember picking up the note, but I can't remember what it said. I'm hoping that maybe the note might still be there, that maybe it fell into the yard somewhere. Can you look for me?"

"Sure thing, child," came Nan's response. "Let me go look around. I'll call you back. Are you calling from Josh's?"

"Yes, but I'm calling from his cell phone...er...which I don't know the number," she apologized.

"No problem. I've got Josh's house number. I'll call that one back."

"Okay." Sabrina exhaled a breath of relief that she might finally be helpful in discovering her attacker. She hoped Nan found that note. Of course, after that hard rain yesterday, it might very well be ruined even if she did find it.

Once she hit the End button on the phone, she saw a "text

message" indicator flashing. She smiled as she pressed the button to retrieve the message. That had been sweet of Josh to think about her yesterday.

When Josh's message popped up, she felt all the blood drain from her face.

Thinking about you. Meet me in the stables.

The familiar phrase flashed through her memory, then came jolting back... *Meet me in the stables.* Those exact same words were on the note the night she was attacked. *God no*! Goose bumps broke out all over her as a shiver shot down her spine. *Had I gone to the stables to meet with Josh? But maybe someone else had written the note.* Her stomach churned. The note had been sitting under a lantern, which Josh mentioned knowing where it hung in the stables. She squeezed her eyes shut. *I was knocked out and left unconscious while the stables were set on fire.*

If it was Josh, why would he do such a thing? Her mind frantically fought to sort through the confused and erratic thoughts tumbling through it. While her heart raced, waves of nausea rolled through her. She felt as if someone had just punched her hard in the gut. Elise had alluded to a bit of rivalry between Josh and Colt. And Josh had pretty much admitted he had a thing for Elise when she'd asked him about it in the hospital...

"Once upon a time...maybe..." he'd said.

Maybe Josh hadn't gotten over Elise like he'd led her to believe and he'd become obsessed? Leaning forward, she put her hands on her knees for support and forced her rapid breathing to slow, even breaths. She'd never felt so betrayed in her life. *No, no, no*! *He said he loved me*, she argued with herself. *Yet you* look *just like Elise.* She shook her head and tried to keep her whirling mind at bay, but snippets of things that Josh had said and done to keep her sequestered, to keep tabs on her whereabouts came slamming back.

"*You don't remember anything else*?" he'd prodded her in the hospital, an urgent look on his face. "*She'll stay with me,*" he'd insisted, refusing to take "no" for an answer.

Was his worry for her insincere? Had he really just been trying to protect himself?

Nan *had* come back early from her dinner, and she said she saw Josh at the stable doors when she arrived. Could it be that he wasn't trying to open them like he claimed, but was caught trying to lock her in, so he had to improvise by pretending to save her?

"*Maybe you were in the wrong place at the wrong time,*" he'd said to her in the hospital. Was he referring to expecting Elise that night?

But if he planned to hurt Elise, why would he leave a note that could be traced back to him behind? She pressed her lips together and closed her eyes. He probably assumed Elise would bring it with her to the stables.

"*...I was hoping to avoid telling you this...to keep you from worrying, but the escaped prisoner has an alibi. It seems he was busy breaking and entering in another house while you were attacked. So that means whoever attacked you is still out there... I don't want you out of my sight any longer than necessary. Your memory could come back at any time.*"

Did he say those things to evoke fear in her? To keep her with him so he'd be the first to know if and when her memory came back? She opened her eyes, trying to rationalize it out.

Yet his declaration that he loved her had appeared so sincere. Either he was the world's best liar or...could it be he regretted what he had done? That, in his efforts to hurt Elise or get back at Colt—whatever his motives that night in the stables—he'd unintentionally fallen in love with her throughout this whole mess? Sabrina couldn't discount that he'd seemed genuinely upset to think Colt was being blamed for the attack on her.

Damn, I'm so confused. Her body shook all over as she took gulps of air and silently prayed, *Please don't let me hyperventilate. I can't pass out now.*

Josh's phone rang, the sudden sound wringing a small cry of alarm out of her. She quickly straightened and almost passed out as her vision blurred. Blinking to regain her equilibrium, she shoved the cell phone in her back pocket, then picked up Josh's cordless phone.

"Hello?"

"It's me." Nan's familiar voice came across the line. "Well, I found a note, but it's just a name and a phone number. This must've been the note that police officer gave you yesterday. Her name was Renee O'Hara, right?"

"Yes, that's her name." Sabrina frowned in confusion. "Hmmm, that's strange because I know I picked up her note after I dropped it..." She trailed off as realization dawned. Sabrina ran over to Josh's bedroom and rummaged in her stuff for her dirty clothes from the day before.

"You there?" Nan asked, her voice sounding worried.

When Sabrina pulled out the note she'd stuck in her jeans pocket yesterday she slowly opened up the crisp paper and then spoke in the phone in a rush of words, "Ohmigod, I had the note from the person who attacked me in my pocket all along. That must've been the note I picked up from underneath the bushes."

"What does it say?"

Sabrina's voice trembled. "Oh, Nan...the note said, *'Elise, meet me in the stables. I've got a couple of things to go over with you.'* It had to have been from Josh. He was scheduled to meet Elise and didn't know she'd left town. I went to the stables to let him know Elise wasn't home. It must've been Josh who attacked me."

"Lord, child! Josh? I can't believe it! Nan said, sounding incredulous.

"I know it sounds crazy, Nan. I can't remember being attacked. All I can remember is reading the note and heading for the stables, and now I have proof I was lead there," she finished with conviction as she tucked the note in her pocket.

Deep hurt knifed through her, but she took a deep breath and straightened her spine, trying to put on a strong front. "I need to call Officer O'Hara right away. Can you please read her number to me?"

"I take it Josh isn't there right now?" Nan asked.

"No, he's gone to pick up his truck that was towed yesterday while he fought a fire in town." With her memory partially returned, her fear spiked. Josh would be returning home soon. She wouldn't be able to pretend nothing was wrong. "I need to get out of here," she said, her voice frantic.

"Colt will be home any minute. I'm going to send him to get you, Sabrina," came the older woman's worried response. "After I give you Officer O'Hara's phone number, hang up and immediately call the police."

She'd just disconnected the call with Nan when someone knocked at the front door. Relief flooded through her. Josh had a key, so there was no way it was him. Setting the cordless phone down on the desk, she walked to the front door and peered around the side windowpane.

A black pickup truck was in the drive and Sabrina was surprised to see Colt's neighbor Jackson Riley at the door. She'd gotten the impression from Josh he didn't like Jackson much, but then could she really trust anything Josh had told her up to this point? At the very least, Jackson might be able to give her a lift back to the Lonestar. The sooner she got out of here, the better.

Opening the door, she said, "Hello, Mr. Riley. I'm sorry, but Josh isn't home at the moment."

"It's about damn time you called the Tanner house. I've been waiting to find out where you were."

12

Sabrina sucked in her breath when Jackson's comment sank in. She glanced at the rope gripped in his hands, shock and disbelief rolling through her as her full memory of the night came flooding back.

The *tone* of his words...the exact same inflection, she'd heard it that night. He'd sounded full of bitterness, lethal and deadly when he'd said, "*Two birds. One stone*," then knocked her out. Her heart jerked and her gaze flew back to his dark, narrowed one.

She tried to slam the door shut, but before she could shut it all the way, he jammed his booted foot between the door and the frame. Gritting her teeth, she put all her weight behind the door, shouldering it as she frantically thought through what she should do if he got inside.

"I want that note. Where is it?" Jackson said through a howl of pain as the door crushed his foot. A second later she felt the door give behind his own shouldering efforts, the door jerking behind his weight. When the door jumped a second time, she knew she couldn't hold him off for long. Sabrina waited a brief second, then let the door go completely and ran.

She glanced back and as she'd hoped, Jackson must've been in the process of ramming the door with his shoulder again when she let it go. He slid across the wood floor while the door slammed open, splintering on its hinges and banging into the wall behind it.

"Take the note," she shrieked, struggling to pull it out of her pocket. Once she got the paper free, she threw it on the floor, hoping the prize he was after would buy her some time. She let out a piercing scream as Jackson barreled across the room, murderous intent stamped on his face.

He only stopped for a second to snatch up the note, then continued to come after her, his expression maniacal. She dashed through the house, clawing a kitchen chair over on its side, then tugging a standing lamp to the floor. She pulled at anything she could think of to slow him down as she made her way to the far side of the house.

She had to get to the back door, she thought frantically as his heavier footfalls sounded close behind. "Get back here, you little bitch," he hissed. "No one is going to get in the way of my goal."

The man was clearly insane! When she made it to the door, her fingers fumbled with the latch, but she finally managed to unlock it. Pulling the door open, she ran across the deck and down the few stairs to the grass.

A rumbling thud sounded behind her as she started for the woods, spurring her to push herself harder. She'd only taken a couple of steps when he shoved her between the shoulder blades and she lost her balance.

Sabrina grunted as she hit the ground hard, the action

bruising her ribs. She screamed as she felt his hand pulling on the waist of her jeans and she quickly rolled onto her back, kicking at him as hard as she could.

Jackson bellowed in anger when she connected with his stomach, knocking him off of her. She sobbed in relief as she rolled to her feet and took off toward the front of the house. With the head start she'd gained, she hoped the house would hide where she entered the woods. She could hide in there until Josh came home.

Josh! If something happened to her, would everyone think it was him? She couldn't let that happen. A new purpose gave her a burst of speed.

Jackson yelling her name when he came around the house had her glancing back for a second. She'd just turned forward when someone stepped out from behind Jackson's truck as she rounded the vehicle.

"Run!" Sabrina screamed, trying to warn the stranger, but as she ran past, the woman quickly stretched her arm out and clotheslined her, slamming her down to the ground.

While Sabrina wheezed to catch her breath, fighting to stay conscious, the voluptuous woman with long blonde hair leaned over and smirked. "Ah, did ya really think you could get away?"

When starbursts flashed before her eyes, Sabrina's last thoughts were of Josh. She felt guilty for thinking he could ever hurt her and angry with herself for being afraid to tell him she loved him. In agonizing slow motion, her vision faded until even the tiny pinpricks of light left behind scattered into nothingness.

Just as Dirk had promised, Josh arrived home in record time. He quickly drove up to his property and frowned at the set of new tire tracks that crushed the taller grass, leading right up to his front door.

When he saw his front door standing wide open, Josh's heart jerked. He dashed out of his truck, his pulse thundering in his ears as he took a flying leap over the four steps to the porch.

"Sabrina!" he yelled as he stepped into his house and faced his worst nightmare.

His front door was broken and the house in shambles as if a fight of some kind had taken place. His gut tense, he hoped and prayed he wouldn't find Sabrina hurt or, God forbid, worse. Once he'd searched every inch of his home and couldn't find her, he stood in the living room, his entire body tense in fear for her safety.

His hands shook as he jammed them through his hair, trying to calm himself into thinking rationally. How the fuck was he going to find her, and *who* the hell was after Sabrina in the first place?

His phone rang, jerking him out of his tumultuous thoughts. Josh picked it up, snarling, "What!

When there was a slight pause on the line, all he could think about was the unknown attacker torturing him with a silent call. "If this is you, you fucking sonofabitch, you'd better not hurt a hair on her head."

"Whoa!" Colt said, his voice calm. "What's going on, Josh?"

Josh shook his head to clear out the enraged thoughts rambling through it and took a steadying breath. "Shit, Colt, I'm sorry. I'm so sorry."

"Hold on, slow down. Take a deep breath and tell me what's going on," he replied in a soothing tone.

"She's gone." Josh's tone lowered. He sat down and put his head in his hand, trying desperately not to lose it. Sabrina needed him now more than ever.

"Sabrina?" Colt asked, his voice lower as if he didn't want someone—more than likely Elise—to overhear their conversation.

"Yes." Josh closed his eyes to keep the tears stinging behind them at bay. Pushing his eyelids hard with his fingers, he opened them and finished, "And I wish to God I knew where to start looking for her."

"Are you sure she didn't leave on her own?"

"What's that supposed to mean?" Josh growled, his head jerking up.

"Calm down, Josh. Nan just received an upsetting call from Sabrina. She found a note that implied you were the person who lured her to the stables the night of the fire."

"What!" Josh yelled into the phone. "I was fighting a fire around the time she was attacked, Colt."

"After today's developments, I have no doubt you're innocent, Josh. I'll be there in two minutes," Colt said firmly.

"Huh? You're here?"

"Hell yeah, I'm home. Someone's trying to fuck with my life and it sounds like yours, too. I've got a pretty damn good idea who'd want to frame me for my own wife's murder," Colt ground out. "No matter what it takes, I'm going to nail the sonofabitch."

"What the hell are you talking about?" Josh asked, his brow furrowing.

"Long story." Colt sighed. "Hang tight. Be at your place in two."

Josh hung up the phone, thankful for Colt's steadying words. Right now, he needed the voice of reason whispering in his ear, because he wasn't going to get there on his own. The thought that Sabrina could think he'd want to do her harm made him physically ill.

While he waited, he realized he should call the police and let them know Sabrina had been kidnapped. He didn't have time to deal with paperwork, waiting for the police and all that bullshit. He'd call Renee and she'd get the ball rolling so he wouldn't have to stop looking for Sabrina on his end.

Standing up, he glanced around the room, looking for his cell phone, since it had Renee's number stored in it. He moved quickly, pushing overturned furniture out of the way, looking underneath couch cushions to see if it had fallen between them. He knew he'd left it at home.

Turning on the cordless phone, he dialed his cell phone at the same time he vowed to always keep the damn thing in the same spot so he didn't lose the phone every five seconds.

The phone rang and rang and that's when he remembered he had left it in vibrate mode. Then a thought struck him, the idea lifting his spirits. Did Sabrina have it? He did ask her to keep it with her. Could he get that lucky?

A steely determination settled over him as he headed for his laptop and pulled up his cell phone provider's website. Clicking on the GPS "locator" link, he punched in his access code and then his phone number and held his breath as the system's "verifying position" icon popped up.

He glanced out the large picture window and saw Colt's

truck drive up and then heard his boots on his porch as the website finally completed its search.

When Colt entered the open door, his gaze moved throughout the house, taking in its torn-up state. Once Colt's blue eyes met his, Josh gave him a humorless, cold smile. He turned his laptop so his neighbor could see the results. "My cell phone locater program." He pointed to an area on the screen. "Sabrina's somewhere in this area." Glancing up at Colt, he continued, "I'm ready to help you fry his ass."

Colt looked at the computer screen, then jerked his knowing gaze back to Josh's. "Jackson Riley. Not at all surprised."

Sabrina awoke to the smell of stale manure and the sensation of something rough yet somewhat cushioned underneath her. When she shifted, the rustle of hay sounded underneath her. Realizing she was unable to move her hands and feet, she panicked as her eyes flew open. Her throat ached and her back hurt, while scratchy ropes bound her wrists and ankles.

Fear shot through her, rolling over her in alternating waves of cold sweat and hair-raising goose bumps. She closed her eyes for a second and did her best to regain some control. When she'd slowed her breathing, she opened her eyes and took in the room surrounding her.

A quick scan of the space with its empty stables told her she was in an abandoned barn. Sunlight streamed through an open window in one of the stalls, nearly blinding her. Tilting her head away from the light, she squirmed, trying to sit up. The hay slid around underneath her and she lost her balance, then fell onto her side. Damn ropes. The way they were tied around her—a short rope connecting her tied wrists to her tied ankles behind her—made it impossible for her to sit herself back up.

"I see you're awake," Jackson commented.

She shifted her gaze to the older man standing by a rough-hewn table against the wall, then quickly surveyed the room, looking for his blonde partner.

"She's not here," he spat, his lip curling in disdain.

"Who?" she asked, sounding raspy.

"May. The bitch who stopped you, then decided to take off, leaving me to clean up this damned mess," he bit out. "It's too bad," he continued as he lifted a sledge hammer the size of a traditional hammer from the table and turned her way. "I was hoping you'd stay unconscious while I finished you off." He examined the hammer, turning its thick metal end in the sunlight, then snorted. "Shooting you would be easiest, but the noise might draw attention, and a knife across the throat is just too messy." He let the hammer's heavy end fall in his palm, a satisfied smile tilting his lips. "A good knock or two or *three* on your skull should do the trick. Nasty work, but it must be done."

Her gaze widened and her heart raced. When she glanced at the hammer and then back to his impassive face, sheer terror gripped her. "Heeeeeeeeelp!" Sabrina tried to scream, but May had really hurt her throat. Her scream came out as a hoarse croak. She didn't let that stop her. She screamed with all she had in her.

"Stop that racket," Jackson said irritably.

When she finally ran out of steam, he lifted the hammer

up and let it fall once more. "You think I'm happy with how this has turned out?"

"I *think* you're a lunatic," she croaked as anger began to overrule her fear. If she was going to die, she wouldn't die begging.

"Damn women. The whole lot of ya," he hissed out in disgust, then set the hammer down on the table to pat his plaid shirt pocket.

"Yeah, but you didn't do this by yourself, did you?" she needled him. She needed to keep him talking. Maybe someone heard her screaming for help.

"You referring to May?" he asked, glancing sharply at her. Pulling a pack of cigarettes from his front pocket, he continued, "May only helped at the tail end of my plan. But she skipped out at the last minute, just like my mole at the insurance agency did when the police started sniffing around. *Which was the whole fucking point*," he bit out, stabbing his finger in the air. "They were *supposed* to come asking questions. She didn't seem to mind taking my five thousand dollars to manipulate records and falsify medical reports. Noooo! But when the heat got too close, 'I'm afraid I'm gonna get caught,'" he mimicked his version of a high-pitched, female voice.

He threw out a few more disparaging obscenities, then continued, "The dumb woman skipped town on me yesterday. Then May, that good-for-nothing woman I thought saw eye-to-eye with me on this whole deal, says, 'See ya on the flip side,' once we arrived back on my property. If I didn't have you to deal with, I'd have taken her out myself just for sheer principle."

He clenched his fist and his face mottled in anger as he

picked up the hammer and slammed it down on the table, cracking the old wood. Witnessing the man's violence firsthand made Sabrina shake. After he struck the table three more times, he took a couple of deep breaths, then he set down the hammer to pull a cigarette out of the pack he'd set on the table. Digging in his jeans pocket, he withdrew a lighter and lit the end.

Jackson took a long, inhaling drag and leaned his head back to stare at the ceiling. It was as if he were waiting for the nicotine to settle him. Several seconds later, his shoulders lost their tension and he dropped the lighter back in his pants pocket.

While he appeared to relax, Sabrina's own nerves had shot to the edge of hysteria. *I don't want to die. Keep him talking. Don't let him have too much time to think.*

"And then there's you." He used his cigarette to point at her, his thick eyebrows slashing downward, gaze narrowed. Smoke came out of his nose and mouth in streams of curling plumes, like an old factory spewing pollution in the air.

"If you hadn't shown up, I wouldn't have mistaken you for Elise that night. I'd have held off, bided my time a bit longer. My tap on Colt's phone line would've allowed me another chance to find a perfect time to frame Colt for his wife's murder."

"You did all this to set Colt up?" she asked, incredulous.

"It was much more than that." He started to pace puffing on his cigarette. Then he paused and continued, smugness in his tone. "I had it perfectly planned. With his wife dead, the police would learn of the life insurance policies he and his wife had taken out on each other—courtesy of May and me—" He stopped and looked at her with an I'm-so-clever smirk, then continued, "In the end, Colt would be arrested for murder."

His face took on a faraway look as if he were picturing the entire scenario he'd just described in his head. "Once Colt was behind bars, if I couldn't find a way to get the land, at least I would know he was suffering."

Her eyebrows drew together in reluctant understanding. The man was clearly mad. But now everything that had happened—her being knocked out, the burned stables, the police's speculation on Colt's life insurance—all made sense.

A satisfied smile tilted the corners of his lips. "Tell me how brilliant I am. How clever and devious. Aren't you impressed?"

"You want me to be impressed by a man who had to depend on others to initiate his master plan?" she said with sarcasm. "For that matter, you couldn't even remember to retrieve your note that lured Elise—or actually *me*—to the stables."

"You were supposed to have brought the note to the stables with you. Would've burned up there." Scowling at her, he stuck the cigarette in the corner of his lips and pulled the note he'd written out of his pocket along with his lighter.

Flicking the lighter open, he lit one corner of the paper and smiled a crooked smirk as he watched it burn to ash.

"No more evidence." He dropped the ball of fire before it reached his fingers, then stomped the burning, charred remains out on the dirt floor beneath his boot.

Her stomach clenched as he dug his boot toe deep in the earth. She had no doubt he planned to "snuff" her out just as easily as he did that paper.

"You talk too much." His gaze met hers after he took another drag on his cigarette. He picked up the hammer and twisted his wrist, the heavy metal head spinning in a deadly circle. "But I'm going to take care of my last loose end." He started toward her, hand fisted on the hammer's handle, a determined look on his face.

Her fear skyrocketed and she tried to jerk herself out of his reach. It's not my time to die, she thought, her mind frantic as primal fear shot through her. "Get the hell away from me," she screamed, her voice fading out.

Jackson squatted beside her and set the hammer down. Taking the cigarette out of his mouth, he grabbed a fistful of her hair and jerked her onto her back.

"I think I'm actually going to enjoy this," he said, his laughter suddenly higher pitched and maniacal.

The fine hairs stood up on her arms at the unbalanced sound while tears stung her eyes from the pain his abusive action caused.

Slowly he wound the fistful of her hair up around his hand, then he seemed to relax as he smoothed the black mass across the hay above her head. "It's a shame I'll have to mar such a pretty face when I bash your skull in," he said in a conversational tone, as if he weren't brutally threatening her.

He picked up the hammer with one hand as he pulled the cigarette out of his mouth with the other and said in a cold tone, "But, pretty or not, you have to go." He raised the hammer.

"I knew you had a screw or two loose, but had no idea you were such a stupid sonofabitch," came a calm, controlled voice from the direction of the doorway to the barn.

As Jackson readjusted his grip on the hammer and stood, Sabrina jerked her gaze toward the voice and let out a sob of relief. Colt stood in the doorway holding a shotgun trained on Jackson.

"Do you really think I'm that dumb? That I wouldn't have

a backup plan, Colt?" Jackson sounded deadly and focused, taking a leisurely puff of his cigarette.

"Put down the hammer, Jackson, or I'll shoot you where you stand," Colt grated. "Give me any excuse to blow a hole in your crazy ass and I'll take it."

Jackson hissed in anger as he dropped the hammer at his feet. Folding one hand behind his back, he growled, "Don't think this is over. I'll never give up," right before he flicked his cigarette into the hay behind Sabrina.

Her heart rate skyrocketed as flames begin to dance on the dry hay behind her head. She tried to squirm away from the heat and that's when she saw Jackson wrap his fingers on the grip of the handgun he'd stuck in his belt behind his back. She tried to warn Colt, but her hoarse voice just cracked instead. When she realized Colt's gaze was on the flames behind her and he wasn't watching Jackson, Sabrina did the only thing she could. She straightened her arms and flattened her palms, then pushed off with her hands and feet, swinging her bent knees toward Jackson, using momentum to slam into his legs as hard as she could.

Jackson stumbled and turned, but still managed to pull his gun, aiming it straight for her head.

Rapid-fire gunshots sounded, knocking the gun from Jackson's hand and sending him to his knees almost simultaneously.

Josh came out of nowhere and rammed Jackson's shoulder with his boot, knocking him onto his side. "You fucking maniac!" he yelled, then quickly kicked Jackson's dropped gun away.

Just as Josh turned to her, Jackson reared up behind him. Coated in blood and full of fury, he dove, grabbing Josh around the waist. While Josh pivoted and swung at Jackson, Sabrina smelled the hay burning and felt the heat all around her. She needed to get out of the raging fire's way, but the bonds around her made rolling out of the way difficult. Sliding away a bit at a time was all she could manage while lying on her side.

Colt had already rushed forth and plowed his fist into Jackson's stomach. "Stay down, you sick bastard!"

Jackson fell onto his back, but even as he wheezed, the older man tried to grab Colt's leg. "I said, stay the hell down," Colt grated, right before he punched Jackson in the jaw, knocking the man out.

"Sabrina!" Josh rushed over to her, concern and fear etched on his face. "Don't move," he ordered, then reached behind her and smothered the flames that had just made their way to her hair.

Scooping her up in his arms, he rushed out of the barn. Colt followed behind them, carrying Jackson's unconscious body.

Once they reached a safe distance from the building, Josh gently laid her down, then quickly cut through the ropes on her wrists and ankles with a knife he retrieved from a holder on his belt. As soon as she was free, he sat down and pulled her in his lap.

Colt dumped Jackson's limp frame on the ground with a hard thud. "Lunatic," he mumbled and shook his head as he looked back at the burning barn.

He approached Sabrina and Josh, then squatted down to search her face with a concerned look. "Are you okay," he asked, touching the scorched ends of her hair.

She nodded, her heart still racing. "I'm fine."

Josh's arms tightened around her. "You're hoarse. God, Sabrina. I'm so sorry this happened."

"How did you find me?" she asked while rubbing her sore wrists.

"My phone's GPS tracker."

She gave a shaky, scratchy laugh and pulled the phone from her back pocket. "I'd forgotten all about it."

Josh took the phone and handed it to Colt. "Do the honors. I'm sure you'll enjoy this. You um, might want to call the ambulance too." Josh shot a look Jackson's way. "He's bleeding pretty good."

While Colt walked away to make the calls, Sabrina looked at Jackson for the first time, then glanced at the gun strapped to Josh's leg. "How many times did you shoot him?"

His eyes narrowed on Jackson, his voice full of steel. "Not nearly enough." Returning his gaze to her, Josh gathered her closer. "I don't know what I would've done if I had lost you, Brina."

She wrapped her arms around his neck, hugging him back. As she breathed in the scents that were all Josh, tears welled and she whispered back, "I'm sorry I thought for even one second you were the one who attacked me."

"There's no reason to apologize. Colt told me about your call to Nan. That note looked pretty damning. She was worried for you until Colt set her straight. Apparently Jackson had someone working for him at the insurance company, helping him set Colt up. Jackson surprised us all at how well he'd manipulated us."

She hugged him tighter. "I still feel bad, but my biggest regret while lying there tied up by Jackson was worrying that I wouldn't get a chance to tell you how I felt about you. I love the man you are, Josh Kelly, and I'm looking forward to learning everything there is to know about you, inside and out. I'm going to stay."

When she finished speaking, Josh quickly pulled back. His gaze full of love, he cupped her face, then winced as his hands connected with her skin.

She grabbed his hands and gasped when she saw the reddened flesh on the tips of his fingers. "Oh, no, your fingers."

"I've had worse. They'll heal." He shrugged the pain away, serious eyes locking with hers. "We've got what matters most. The rest we'll figure out, okay?"

The last he'd said with a reassuring smile. She knew he referred to his firefighting. She smiled back, nodding in agreement, then snuggled close and rubbed her nose against his chest, thankful to be in his arms once more.

THREE DAYS LATER, Elise finished combing through Sabrina's wet hair, then separated a hank and held the scissors to it. "You ready?" she asked, her green eyes glassy with unshed tears.

Elise had done nothing but shower her with attention since Josh brought her to the Lonestar after he and Colt had rescued her from Jackson. So far she'd taken her shopping, to the movies, out to Rockin' Joes, and out to dinner two nights in a row. She'd wanted to take Sabrina to a salon to have her hair done, but Sabrina just pulled it into a bun, refusing the offer. She'd finally let Elise convince her to part with the damaged locks. Sabrina came back to the present and exhaled the breath she'd been holding. "Yes."

When Elise snipped off four inches, tears started falling down her cheeks. "I'm so sorry, Sabrina."

"Stop crying, Elise. It's okay."

Elise shook her head, tears streaming faster now. "This is all my fault."

"It's not your fault. It's Jackson's." Sabrina grabbed her hand. "And, seriously. I want you to stop crying. Otherwise, you won't cut in a straight line."

Elise met her gaze and snickered. "Oh. Good point." Brushing away her tears with the back of her hand, she squared her shoulders, then lifted another wet hank and took a deep breath. "Let's get back to it."

While Elise cut the burned ends of her hair, she said, "Colt called and said the police have caught and arrested the woman from the insurance agency."

"That's great!" Sabrina met Elise's gaze in the mirror, smiling.

Elise nodded and combed through her hair to get to the next section. "Now if they could just find and arrest May Winston, I'll be ecstatic."

Sabrina frowned. "I can't believe this woman did this to get back at Colt for firing her."

Elise pursed her lips in annoyance. "I didn't tell you the whole story. Beyond the fact that she's an unhappy ex-employee of Colt's rodeo, May believes Colt jilted her too."

Sabrina's eyebrows shot up. "Jilted? As in she and Colt were lovers?"

Elise nodded. "It was over a long time ago, way before Colt and I met. But May always held out hope they'd get back together."

"Ah, then Colt laid eyes on you..." Sabrina filled in the missing pieces.

"Yep, and that was the end of May's hopes to be the future Mrs. Colt Tanner." Elise grinned her satisfaction as she snipped the last burned strand, evening up her hair.

As she began to blow dry Sabrina's hair, Nan poked her head in the bathroom doorway. "Josh just called. He said, 'Tell Elise I'm picking Sabrina up in two hours.'"

Josh was coming to pick her up? Sabrina's heart raced in excitement.

Elise waved the hairbrush in the air. "Why did Josh tell you to tell me?" She frowned in confusion. "For that matter, why didn't he ask Sabrina if she wanted to go?"

"Sabrina wants to go!" Sabrina said quickly, giving her a wide grin. She'd missed Josh terribly these past few days, but she'd also needed to spend some quality time with her friend.

After Nan left, Elise pursed her lips, eyeing her. "Are you sure you're okay?"

Sabrina nodded. "Yes. If you could help me style my hair, I have a couple phone calls to make before he gets here."

13

Nervous butterflies danced in Sabrina's stomach when a knock sounded at the front door.

Elise glanced up from her mug of coffee, eyebrow arched. "Well, aren't you going to answer it?"

Sabrina gave her a big hug, then practically ran to the front door, Elise's laughter floating behind her. "Hush," she hissed toward the kitchen, before she straightened her button down shirt over her belted jeans, then opened the door.

She barely had a chance to soak in Josh's sexy five o'clock shadow, his forest green button down shirt or dark Wranglers before he immediately pulled her against his chest and wrapped his arms around her.

"Three days was all I could handle," he whispered huskily against her temple, his cowboy hat shielding her face from the afternoon sun.

Sabrina hugged his waist and pressed her nose into his chest, inhaling his masculine scent of leather and all male. "I've missed you too, especially the way you smell."

His hand slid down her back, resting at the base of her spine. "Are you ready to go?"

She nodded.

Once they got in his truck, Sabrina turned to Josh and flipped her shoulder-length hair. "What do you think? Elise cried as she cut off the burned ends. Tomorrow she's going to take me to a salon so they can shape it properly."

Josh removed his hat and set it on the seat. His teal gaze shifted to the color of a churning ocean as he threaded his fingers through the shorter strands. "Every time I think about how close I came to losing you..." He paused, his jaw muscle jumping before he continued in a controlled voice, "It's a good thing Jackson's in jail and out of my reach."

Charmed by his protective tone and gentle touch, she grabbed his wrist and laced her fingers with his. Tracing the pads of her fingers over the mostly healed burns on his fingers, she kissed the ones that still looked a bit pink. "I'm fine. My very own hero was there to save me."

"About that..." Josh laid his wrist on the steering wheel and let his gaze scan the open prairie for a second. When his gaze met hers once more, the heat and love behind it made her heart melt. "I've decided to change my firefighting status."

Surprised by his announcement, she squeezed his hand but couldn't help the guilt that washed over her. "How have you changed it? You're not quitting are you, Josh?"

"Is that what you want?"

She shook her head, her stomach churning. "Not for me. Never for me."

He released her hand and traced a finger down the side of her face. "I saved you from a fire once. That was hard enough when you were a beautiful stranger I'd just met. But when I saw those flames come close to the woman I deeply love the other day, I realized exactly how you felt when you thought I might not come home from fighting that fire. It terrified the shit out of me."

"So you're quitting." She looked down and the tears fell, her shoulders slumping. One day he'd resent her for being the reason he stopped fighting fires. That's the last thing she wanted.

Josh touched her chin, lifting it until she had to meet his gaze. "When it comes to you, I'm not willing to take as many risks, but no, I'm not quitting, I'm just shifting direction. Following the investigation with Renee really interested me, so I've decided to get my fire investigator certification and work on cases for the fire department on a part-time basis. And yes, my name will still be on the emergency call list as a last resort firefighter."

She felt a slight twinge that he'd still be fighting fires, even rarely, but if he could try to find a middle ground, so could she. She took a deep breath and smiled. "I'm glad you'll still be involved in something you feel so strongly about, but," she paused, confused. "Why are you only going part-time as an investigator?"

His expression turned serious. "Every time I investigate or fight a fire, I'll still be fighting for Nick, but now I want to fight for my own happiness. I've put off what I've always wanted to do for too long. Those empty stalls you saw in my stables? They'll soon be full. My father's jumping up and down with glee that I'm finally joining the family business of raising horses. He's already bushwhacked a clean path from the Double K up to my house."

She sniffed back her tears and clasped his hand, needing to

know his decision was his and his alone, "What you've always *wanted* to do?"

He nodded. "Yeah."

When she smiled, he reached into his back pocket. "Speaking of something I want..." He lifted her right hand in the air. "Hold your hand there for a sec."

Sabrina did as he asked, dying of curiosity.

Josh slid a thin tan string around the bottom of her third finger on her right hand, saying, "I might not always give you what you want—"

"Josh wait!" She curled her fingers around the string, stopping him. The look of hurt in his eyes made her heart beat faster. She quickly replaced her right hand with her left, laying it over the string still hanging between his fingers. "It needs to be the *right* hand."

Tender heat swirled in Josh's eyes as he slid the string around the third finger on her left hand and tied it in a bow, saying, "But I promise to always give you what you need."

Sabrina had never felt so much love. Josh was making a promise about their relationship, but the string also reminded her how deeply he'd looked. He knew what made her happy or sad, knew what turned her on, and most importantly he never let her shy away from the fact they were meant to be. Jeremy had squandered their time together, proving quantity didn't count for much, but Josh had made the most of their stolen moments, showing her that quality mattered more than anything.

Josh's warm fingers clasped her hand and he pressed a kiss to the bow on her finger. "I love you, Sabrina."

She folded her hand around his, emotion clogging her

throat. "I love you too Josh. I think I have from the moment you said, 'Elise who?'"

When Josh barked out a laugh, she snickered, then sobered. "I have something for you too. But it's at your house."

"My house *is* your house." Grinning, Josh started his truck.

As he turned onto the cut-out path his dad had made from the Double K up to his house, Josh asked, "Do you think your boss would let you work from home?"

She pulled her gaze away from the gorgeous woods streaming by, eyebrows raised. There's no way he could've known that she'd hinted at this idea with her boss when she called and asked to take a couple extra days off. After her boss heard what happened to her, he was more than willing to let her take the time she needed. "I think my boss would go for a proposal for me to telecommute so long as I came back to Arizona a few times a year for meetings and such. It'll probably take me a week or so to relocate my office," she mused, thinking about everything she'd need to do to move.

"That's great." Josh nodded, his brow furrowed in concentration. "We can get any office equipment you'll need."

"Once I get it set up in my new apartment—"

"Your apartment?" Josh shot her a frown. "I was sincere about my place being yours, Brina. I want you with me. I promise you'll have the space you need to get your work done from home."

The man was pure temptation. "Josh...let's talk about that later."

Glancing at her with serious eyes, he grumbled, "These past three days have been pure torture. Colt told me to stow it every time I tried to call."

She couldn't help the smile that spread across her face. "You called?"

"Hell yeah, I called. Every day, but he kept blocking me." Josh let out a dark, satisfied laugh. "Then he came by the Double K last night, looking as surly as I've felt since I had to leave you with them and said, "I want my wife back. You can call Sabrina tomorrow."

Sabrina laughed. "You tough cowboys sure can't seem to live without your women."

Josh stopped the truck in front of his house and cut the engine, flashing a wide smile. "Damn straight!" Once she followed him out of his truck, he put his arm around her shoulders and said, "When a cowboy finds his woman, he never lets her go, sweetheart. Not even for a few days." His amusement settled as they mounted the steps. "So what did you have to give me?"

Sabrina grabbed the box wrapped in brown paper leaning against his front door and tucked it under her arm. "Go on in and stand in the living room, facing the kitchen."

He glanced at the box, brow furrowed. "Where'd that come from? It wasn't there when I left."

She shooed him on. "Go on and just do as I ask."

Josh shrugged and entered the living room. Turning to face the kitchen, he folded his arms. Sabrina was right behind him, but as she started to pull off the paper, he turned his shoulder.

"Uh, Josh. It's a surprise! Turn around. And close your eyes this time."

With a heavy sigh, he grinned, then turned and closed his eyes. "Shut now."

Sabrina ripped off the paper and smiled at the large shadow box frame. Nan's sister had done a fantastic job with the framing, and so had all the other people she'd enlisted to help her with this project.

She carefully lifted it up and set it on the mantel. Moving a horse statue to the left and a clock to the right, she placed the shadow box in the middle of the mantel and stood back, suddenly nervous. What if Josh hated it? It had seemed like such a good idea at the time. Biting her lip, she moved to stand beside Josh and took a deep breath. "You can turn around now."

Josh didn't say anything as he turned and stared at the shadow box. His throat worked and emotions flickered across his face so quickly, she wasn't sure what he was thinking. When he walked right up to the frame, his steps fast, his stance tense, she followed and twisted her hands together, worried she'd royally screwed up. "You hate it, don't you?"

Sabrina had taken that old picture of him and Nick and put it in its own small frame inside a shadow box. The fact she'd taken the time to do this floored him. All kinds of emotions rolled through him; sadness for Nick's death, regret for the man he'd never become, happiness that he'd met Sabrina, and thankfulness that she knew just how to burrow straight through to his heavy heart and set it free.

The picture frame was set back in the left half of the shadow box. His Colt 45 rested upright in a stand in front of the picture frame but centered in the shadow box. The gun's metal was shined up and new looking. No more dust. *Wait? Was it my gun?* He stepped up to the frame and tilted his head to see. No, it was Nick's gun. When he straightened, his gaze landed on the engraving on the silver plaque in the back right half of the box. The title read: *Future Heroes*. Underneath the title in smaller script, it read: Sabrina Gentry and a date. His eyes watered a little when he recognized the date Sabrina had engraved. It was three days ago.

Sabrina's small hand on his arm drew him back to his surroundings. "Do you hate me?" she asked, lips trembling slightly, gorgeous green eyes wide with worry. "I wanted you to know, and Nick too, that he did become the hero he'd always wanted to be. It might've been your shooting skills that saved me, but it was his gun, Josh. Nick's gun."

Josh's chest ached and he found it hard to breathe. He pulled the woman he loved into his arms, gathering her close. She'd become so precious to him, he couldn't imagine his life without her. His voice was hoarse with emotion, but he managed to get the words out, "Nick would've loved you, Sabrina."

Relief flooded through her that Josh seemed happy with his gift. She wrapped her arms around his waist and laid her head on his chest. "Your gun is clean and in its holster where it belongs."

Josh cupped her face and looked into her eyes. "I love the shadow box. I can't even put into words what it means to me. Thank you," he finished, pressing his lips to hers in a tender kiss.

When she started to kiss him back, Josh quickly stepped back, a broad smile on his lips. "I'll be right back. Sit down on the couch and wait for me."

Perplexed, Sabrina did as he asked, sinking into the soft cushions.

When Josh returned, he sat down beside her and clasped her hand in his. Goose bumps formed on her arms as he ran his thumb along the string he'd tied earlier. Then he surprised her by sliding a two-carat sapphire flanked by trillion cut diamonds on her finger. "I guessed at your size...will you marry me, Brina? You don't have to say yes right away, but I can't stand another day going by without asking you to spend the rest of your life with me."

Her chest hurt with the love she felt for this amazing man. Big tears welled and she nodded. "Yes, I'll marry you." Josh flashed a wide smile and started to untie the string, but she yanked her hand back. "No, I want it to wear off. Once it's gone, we'll set a date. That should be long enough to convince my mom that I'm not crazy for marrying a man I just met."

"Fine," Josh said grudgingly as he pulled her back against his chest and settled her ring hand on his thigh.

A quiet settled between them while he fiddled with her ring, pushing it back and forth along her finger. She snuggled deeper into his warm embrace. "What are you thinking?"

"I'm thinking that I wished I'd used thread or something equally fragile when I tied that damn string on your finger."

He sounded so disgruntled, she patted his cheek, then stood and faced him. "There are plenty of activities we can do that'll eventually wear it out."

Josh sat up, his gaze hungrily sweeping over her body. "Like sweaty exercise?"

She started backing up toward the bedroom. "That's one. Then there are showers. Lots of lonnnng showers," she finished, crooking her finger.

"*Lots* can only happen if you're here, Brina." His expression turned serious, tension setting in his shoulders. "Say you'll move in with me."

She loved him, deeply and irrevocably. She wouldn't want to be apart from him either. When she nodded, Josh bolted off the couch and had scooped her up over his shoulder before she could turn and run.

As he rushed her into the bedroom, Sabrina squealed in delight and smacked at his muscular butt. "Put me down, Josh Kelly."

"Happy to oblige, ma'am!" He dropped her onto the bed and swiftly pulled her hands over her head. Easing down on top of her, he pressed his jean-covered erection against her heated center. "You know, these gorgeous hands of yours seem to be pinned or tied quite often. Be a shame if that string should suddenly snap or get snipped while you're bound."

Sabrina sucked in a breath and tugged to free her arms. "You wouldn't dare."

His teal gaze glittered with ruthless intent, his fingers squeezing hers tighter. "But I do dare, Brina. I dare all kinds of things, and you wouldn't have it any other way."

She shook her head, eyes glistening with emotion. "But not this, Josh. Let it wear off. Please."

His expression softened and his hold loosened slightly. "It means that much to you?"

She nodded. "Right now the only thing binding us together is our word, not a piece of paper like marriage will. That's what the string represents to me. I want it to wear out and let if fall off naturally."

Josh sighed heavily, then lowered his lips to hers. She was surprised when his kiss wasn't anything like the calm image he'd projected. He captured her lips, thrusting his tongue deep into her mouth, instantly stealing her breath with his aggressiveness.

Squirming, she rocked her hips and pressed against him, saying between kisses, "I'm sure we'll do our best to help it along."

He moved his warm mouth to her throat, a sinful chuckle rumbling against her skin. "You've just issued a challenge. I hope you're prepared for very little sleep, baby."

"Josh, that's not what I meant," she said between gasps as he nipped at the swell of her breast above her bra.

He lifted his head, eyes churning with emotion. "The string represents a binding commitment. I'm going to show you just how much." A wicked grin flashed. "It'll be worn ragged in no time."

I HOPE you enjoyed Josh and Sabrina's story. If you found *Josh's Justice* an entertaining and enjoyable read, I hope you'll take the time to leave a review and share your thoughts with others on the on-line store where you purchased it. Your review could help other readers decide to give Josh's story a try!

*If you love the sexy banter and alpha heroes in my **BAD IN BOOTS** series, turn the page to check out a brief excerpt from book one, MISTER BLACK, in my **New York Times** and **USA Today** best selling contemporary romance **IN THE SHADOWS** series. MISTER BLACK is the only novella. All the other books in the series are novel length. Happy reading!*

ALL FUTURE BOOKS will be released under the P.T. Michelle name, but with the same irresistible characters and stories you've come to expect from my books. To make sure you don't miss any new P.T. Michelle releases, be sure ***to sign up for my newsletter here:*** bit.ly/11tqAQN

MISTER BLACK - EXCERPT

IN THE SHADOWS SERIES

Check out a brief excerpt from book one, MISTER BLACK, in my ***New York Times*** *and* ***USA Today*** *best selling contemporary romance* ***IN THE SHADOWS*** *series.*

Straightening, Sebastian takes off his belt and shirt. His breathing saws in and out as he stares down at me for a beat before removing his mask. I'm glad to know I'm not the only one affected. The outline of his broad shoulders and hard, fit body make me want to explore every dip and hollow with my tongue. I'm sad that it's too dark to see more than bits of light play on his face from trees moving in the wind outside, but that means he can't really see mine either.

I reach up and remove my mask. I want to kiss him without it in the way. I don't want anything between us. We'll just hide in the shadows instead.

"Your name," he says, his tone demanding compliance.

I pull my dress over my head, tossing it to him.

My answer.

He crushes the material in a tight fist, then drops it to the floor. Reaching for my ankles, he encircles them, fingers flexing on my skin. Distant lightning flashes, briefly highlighting the top half of his face. The room goes dark again, and all I can picture is the near feral look in his amazing eyes as he tugs me toward him with a powerful jerk, his tone gravelly and full of want. "Then I'll just call you *Mine.*"

When he runs his hands up the inside of my thighs, pressing them to the bed with a quiet order, "Keep them here," I comply, eager anticipation curling in my belly. I'm exposed, but he's already seen the ugliest side of me. When I was raw and at my weakest. He just doesn't know it.

Check out Mister Black!

OTHER BOOKS BY P.T. MICHELLE

In the Shadows

(Contemporary Romance, 18+)

Mister Black (Book 1 - Talia & Sebastian)

Scarlett Red (Book 2 - Talia & Sebastian)

Blackest Red (Book 3 - Talia & Sebastian)

Gold Shimmer (Book 4 - Cass & Calder)

Steel Rush (Book 5 - Cass & Calder)

Black Platinum (Book 6 - Talia & Sebastian)

Reddest Black (Book 7 - Talia & Sebastian) - Late Fall 2017

Brightest Kind of Darkness Series

(YA/New Adult Paranormal Romance, 16+)

Ethan (Prequel)

Brightest Kind of Darkness (Book 1)

Lucid (Book 2)

Destiny (Book 3)

Desire (Book 4)

Awaken (Book 5)

Other works by P.T. Michelle writing as Patrice Michelle

Bad in Boots series
(Contemporary Romance, 18+)
Harm's Hunger
Ty's Temptation
Colt's Choice
Josh's Justice

Kendrian Vampires series
(Paranormal Romance, 18+)
A Taste for Passion
A Taste for Revenge
A Taste for Control

Stay up-to-date on her latest releases:

Join P.T's Newsletter:
http://bit.ly/11tqAQN

Visit P.T. :

Website: http://www.ptmichelle.com
Twitter: https://twitter.com/PT_Michelle
Facebook: https://www.facebook.com/PTMichelleAuthor
Instagram: http://instagram.com/p.t.michelle
Goodreads:
http://www.goodreads.com/author/show/4862274.P_T_Mic
helle

P.T. Michelle's Facebook Readers' Group:
https://www.facebook.com/groups/PTMichelleReadersGrou
p/

ABOUT THE AUTHOR

P.T. Michelle is the *NEW YORK TIMES*, *USA TODAY*, and International Bestselling author of the New Adult contemporary romance series IN THE SHADOWS, the YA/New Adult crossover series BRIGHTEST KIND OF DARKNESS, and the romance series: BAD IN BOOTS, KENDRIAN VAMPIRES and SCIONS (listed under Patrice Michelle). She keeps a spiral notepad with her at all times, even on her nightstand. When P.T. isn't writing, she can usually be found reading or taking pictures of landscapes, sunsets and anything beautiful or odd in nature.

To learn when the next P.T. Michelle book will release, join P.T.'s free newsletter http://bit.ly/11tqAQN

Follow P.T. Michelle

www.ptmichelle.com

Made in the USA
Middletown, DE
16 February 2022

61327206R00130